# A TASTE OF HAPPINESS

When Giselle Anderson gives up her dream of working in one of Paris's best known restaurants and goes instead to build up her father's newly-acquired restaurant on an island off the west coast of France, she intends it to be a short-term project. Her father's business partner, Jean Claude Morville, makes it very clear that he is not going to be a silent partner — but will Giselle be able to work alongside this charismatic man and still feel free to walk away when summer is over?

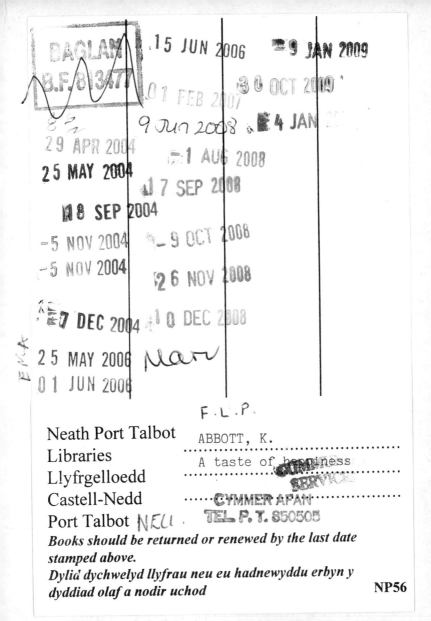

**Neath Port Talbot Libraries Llyfrgelloedd Castell-Nedd Port Talbot**

*Books should be returned or renewed by the last date stamped above.*

*Dylia dychwelyd llyfrau neu eu hadnewyddu erbyn y dyddiad olaf a nodir uchod*

NP56

KAREN ABBOTT

# A TASTE
# OF
# HAPPINESS

*Complete and Unabridged*

# LINFORD
*Leicester*

First published in Great Britain in 2002

First Linford Edition
published 2004

British Library CIP Data

Abbott, Karen
    A taste of happiness.—Large print ed.—
Linford romance library
    1. Love stories
    2. Large type books
    I. Title
    823.9′14 [F]

    ISBN 1–84395–264–5

Published by
F. A. Thorpe (Publishing)
Anstey, Leicestershire

Set by Words & Graphics Ltd.
Anstey, Leicestershire
Printed and bound in Great Britain by
T. J. International Ltd., Padstow, Cornwall

This book is printed on acid-free paper

# 1

It was still dark when Giselle Anderson first opened her eyes on the last day of November. She lay still for a moment, wondering why there was a suppressed excitement surging deep within her. Then she remembered.

Today, she would get the final results of her Catering Diploma Course and, resting on that result, the confirmation of six months' training, starting early in December under Paul Verlaine, the renowned Master Chef at his well-known restaurant in Paris.

She lay back on her pillow with a contented sigh. It was what she had worked towards for the past three and a half years, and now it was within her grasp. Her greatest satisfaction was that she had done it on her own, without any of her father's well-intentioned boosts up the catering ladder. Tom

Anderson couldn't understand why his only daughter didn't want to get into the trade through the back door.

'You need all the help and name-dropping available,' he had tried to persuade her. 'You'll ride to the top twice as quickly, and it'll give you more time to settle down and give me some grandchildren before I'm too old to enjoy them!'

'Dad!' she had exclaimed incredulously. 'How chauvinistic can you get? I don't want to settle down and have babies! Not for a long time yet! I'm only twenty-two!'

He was a fine one to talk, she reflected! He hadn't married until he was twenty-nine and she hadn't appeared until five years later. Francine, her mother, was seven years younger, a vivacious French woman with dark curly hair, a slim, petite figure and a face that had bowled her dad over the first time they met twenty-six years ago. They had made a good partnership until Francine had died tragically of cancer six months ago.

Giselle's mood sobered at the memory. It had shaken them both, but her dad was devastated. He had aged visibly and lost much of his vigour in the past few months. Was that why he had decided to uproot himself and buy a failing restaurant on Ile D'Oleron, a small island off the southwest coast of France? It was where her mother had been born, where she grew up and she had returned there at least twice a year. As a family, they had spent a number of holidays there. Giselle's favourite times had been spring, before the summer visitors had arrived and autumn, once they had gone.

Situated on the fringe of the Bay of Biscay, the island enjoyed a Mediterranean climate, where tall hollyhocks in all shades of pinks and reds and cream grew wild. On its seaward side, the Atlantic waves came rolling in, attracting surfers from all over the world. Its fishing ports were worked by local fishermen, bringing their varied catch daily to the local markets.

Tom Anderson had been disappointed when Giselle chose to accept Paul Verlaine's offer over his own. He missed his wife more than Giselle realised and Giselle was so much like her, except that her long tawny hair was straighter. She generally wore it loose, with a few strands tucked behind her ears, but when at work in the kitchen she coiled it up on top of her head or tied it casually in a ponytail.

Her smoky eyes had looked impassionately at her father.

'It will mean more, Dad,' she had reasoned fervently, unaware of how hurt he had been. 'I'll have Paul Verlaine's name behind me. It will take me anywhere!'

She sighed now and pushed away her guilty thoughts. She had her own life to lead, and didn't want to trail in her father's illustrious footsteps. It was Paris that called her, not Ile D'Oleron! With that thought uppermost in her mind, she pushed back her duvet and swung her legs out of bed. Warm shower, get dressed, and drive over to the college. This day was going to change her life for ever, and she wanted to get on with it!

She arrived at the college at the same time as her friends. They had agreed to meet up and discover their results together. They had been together for more than three years and planned to celebrate their dividing of ways in grand style that evening. With linked arms, the four of them made their way to the main corridor outside the bursar's office and joined the large group of students already gathered there, eagerly searching the lists for their own name, and knew relief and exultation when they found them! All four had passed with excellent grades.

They spun round and hugged each other, exclaiming their joy.

'London, here I come!' Simon declared. 'I'm starting right away, on the run-up to Christmas. I'll get a good bonus that way! I might even send you all a Christmas present!'

'That'll be a first!' Giselle laughed. 'I didn't even get a card last year!'

'I've nothing lined up,' Melanie Foster pouted. 'I didn't think I'd pass!'

She was the least motivated of their group. With two doting parents who gave her everything she asked for, a job wasn't high on her priority list.

'Silly goose! You'll find something somewhere, if you start looking!' Giselle tried encouraging her. 'No-one will come knocking on your door with a job, that's for sure!'

She turned to the other of their foursome, Daniel Roberts.

'What about you, Daniel? Will you take that job in Manchester?'

Daniel nodded, putting his arm round her shoulders.

'Yes, I guess so. I wish you were coming with me. You know they would take you as well. Won't you change your mind?'

'What, and give up Paris? Are you mad? No chance!'

She hesitated as his face fell.

'I'm sorry. I didn't mean to upset you.'

She reached up and touched his face lightly. They had been close over the last few months, but that was as far as she wanted it to go. As she had told her dad, she didn't want to settle down yet, and Daniel was getting to take her too much for granted, expecting her to drop her other friends and go out solely with him. She'd be glad of the break.

'It's only six months, anyway,' she added, by way of consolation.

'And then you'll come back?' Daniel pressed.

Giselle shrugged her shoulders. He was trying to pin her down and she didn't want that!

'I'll have to see how it goes. You never know what might come along next.'

'That's what I'm afraid of. Let's get engaged before you go. Then we'll belong to each other, and the break won't be final!'

Giselle fell silent and turned away.

She didn't want to see the eagerness in his face. She sighed, more in exasperation than anything else.

'We've gone through all this before, Daniel. My answer still stands. I'm not ready! I want to spread my wings a bit. I want to try something different.'

She knew she had disappointed him, but that was his own fault. Why couldn't he accept her refusal?

'Come on, you two!' Simon was calling. 'Everyone's going to the coffee bar, and we'll make our plans for this evening! It's going to be a rave-up!'

Thankful of the diversion, Giselle broke away.

'We're coming! And then I must ring Dad to tell him the good news.'

She knew he'd be glad for her, even though she wasn't joining him, and he was! His little girl had done well. Like father, like daughter!

'When are you coming home?' he asked.

'At the weekend. You can take me out to that new restaurant in town! Let's see if we could do anything better!'

He laughed.

'I'll bet we could!'

Later that day, Giselle and Melanie left the small flat they shared and went by bus to the local night club where they had arranged to meet the boys and some other students on their course. Everyone was in high spirits. None of their particular class had failed, so there was nothing to mar their joy.

It was late when she and Melanie arrived back at their flat, and immediately she could see the light on the answer phone flashing.

'Get that, will you, Mel? I'll put the kettle on for some coffee.'

She hummed one of the tunes they had danced to as she filled the kettle. It had been a good evening, and Daniel had seemed resigned to her wish to cool their relationship for a while. A surge of excitement flowed through her as she thought of Paris. This time next week she would be there! She plugged in the kettle and turned back to Melanie, seeing at once that something was wrong. Melanie's face had gone pale.

'What is it?' Giselle asked, suddenly apprehensive.

'Oh, Giselle!'

Melanie put her hand to her mouth, her eyes wide.

'There's no easy way to say this. Your dad's been in an accident. He's unconscious, and they want you at the hospital as soon as you can make it.'

They were there within the half hour. Melanie had insisted on accompanying her and Giselle was glad of her company. Hospitals weren't the most congenial places to be, especially when someone you loved was lying unconscious and hovering between life and death on a trolley in the accident and emergency department.

Someone had brought them a cup of coffee and Giselle drank it without even knowing she had done so. Her mind was in turmoil. Her dad couldn't die! He just couldn't! She needed him! He was all the family she had, in this country, at least.

'Don't die, Dad!' she whispered to him.

She squeezed his hand, willing him to open his eyes, but he didn't, not that day, nor the next!

Giselle walked around in a daze. Somehow, every night, she went back home, and somehow, the next day, she returned to the hospital to sit at her father's bedside, waiting for some sign that he was going to come out of the coma. She knew she must have phoned Paul Verlaine's restaurant in Paris, though she had no clear recollection of doing so. Melanie told her that they were keeping the position open for her for the time being but that she must do what she felt was right for her father and herself.

Giselle just shook her head. She couldn't make decisions right now. She didn't know what was going to happen.

Daniel had been round. He tried to comfort her, offered to stay with her, even invited her to Manchester with him. Giselle's mind refused to function.

'I'll be all right!' she kept assuring him. 'Dad'll be out of his coma soon, and then I'll be able to decide what to do.'

Within a week, Tom's condition stabilised. He looked smaller, somehow, a fearful sight with all the tubes and wires that led to him and from him but the doctors assured her that he was in no pain and that there was still a chance that he could come out of the coma and make some degree of recovery.

Christmas came. Giselle refused all invitations that would take her away from her dad's bedside for more than an hour. She went to a Christmas Day service in the hospital chapel, praying with all her might for a sign of recovery from her dad. She returned to the ward, where he lay still. Every so often, two nurses would turn him slightly, to relieve the pressure points. Giselle wiped his face with damp cloths. It was just before tea-time. The carol singers had been, the Christmas tree at home was bare of presents and Giselle was wondering whether or not to leave for the day. She leaned nearer to her father's head.

'I'm going now, Dad. I'll be back tomorrow. Happy Christmas!'

She lowered her head and dropped a kiss on his forehead then drew back to look at him. His eyes, closed for so long, opened. He seemed to look straight at her, though no muscles of his face moved and his eyes stared blankly.

'Dad?'

An incredible joy swept through her. He was coming round! She whirled round and called to the nurse.

'Nurse! Nurse! Come quickly! Dad's just opened his eyes!'

The nurse hurried over, but Tom's eyes had closed again. The nurse picked up his wrist, testing his pulse. She laid his hand down. His eyes remained closed but Giselle was sure he looked different.

'It often happens,' the nurse explained kindly. 'It may be a sign that he is coming round but it's difficult to tell. Go home. We'll let you know if anything happens.'

Giselle decided to do as she said. She was tired, but also felt buoyed up by the small sign of recovery. She had asked for a sign, and it had been given, but what was she now to do? Should she stay around as she had been doing? What would her dad want her to do?

Daniel was in no doubt when he called her on Boxing Day.

'He's probably telling you to get on with your life, but to stay nearby,' he added, softly, trying to pull her closer.

She knew he meant Manchester. Giselle thought for a moment. She could see a scene in her mind's eye. The sky was blue, the land low, the leaves of tall trees rustled in the fresh breeze. The sun was shining and the fragrance of flowers wafted past her nostrils.

'I'm going to France!' she said abruptly.

'France?' Daniel said, looking dazed. 'Of course, that's exactly what your father wanted!' he added sarcastically.

'I don't mean Paris,' Giselle said gently. 'I mean Ile D'Oleron and the restaurant he's bought!'

That was what her father had wanted! She would go to Ile D'Oleron. She would do what her dad had planned to do! She would build up the restaurant and, when he recovered, he could take over and live out his life in the place where he had met his wife so long ago. She looked Daniel straight in the eyes.

'I'm going to Ile D'Oleron,' she repeated firmly. 'I'm going to build up Dad's dream for him. It's what he wanted me to do, and I'll do it!'

# 2

Once the idea had taken root, Giselle couldn't wait to put it into action. She wrote to her mother's Uncle Thierry, who had always given them a welcome on their holiday visits, telling him of the developments and of her proposed line of action. He cabled back with his condolences over Tom's accident and said he would be in touch with her later.

She made all the necessary arrangements at the hospital, packed her share of the household items in the flat into a self-drive van and took them to her father's house, which she arranged to close up for six months, asking a neighbour to keep a check on it.

She made an appointment to see her bank manager to arrange overseas access to her bank account then left a forwarding address at the post office, and told all her friends where she was going. Most of them thought she was mad and taking on far more than she could manage, but they wished her well. Daniel was the only one who tried to persuade her to change her mind.

'It's a stupid idea!' he protested. 'You've said yourself you don't know exactly where this place is that he's bought, or what it's like! It could be a pile of rubbish! If it was already failing, how do you know you can build it up again? What if it needs heavy manual labour?'

'Let me tell you, Daniel Roberts, I've got what it takes! If Dad had the vision to take it on, then I can do it, too! Anyway, it's all irrelevant, all these arguments against me going! I've already booked my ticket on the ferry. I'll send you a postcard!'

Her final visit to the hospital wasn't easy. During the past week she had talked to her dad about her plans but she didn't know if he could hear her.

She had been told that people in a coma could often hear everything that was said to them, so she did talk at length. It helped her to sort out her ideas and make some plans about where to start.

'So, I'll not be coming to see you for a while, Dad, but I know you'll understand. I'll send you a tape every so often, telling you what I've been doing and one of the nurses will play it to you. You can come and join me as soon as you're better! That will be nice, won't it?'

Her voice broke. What if he didn't get better? She couldn't face that possibility. He would get better! He would! A tiny tear trickled down her cheek as she leaned over to kiss him. She couldn't be sure, but she felt there was a softening around his mouth as she looked at him, as if he was trying to smile. She kissed him again.

'I love you, Dad. See you soon!'

★  ★  ★

It was the worst Channel crossing she had ever made, probably because it was far earlier in the year than her usual holiday trips. She had never been until May before, when the winter storms were over. The crossing to St Malo was an overnight one and the estimated arrival in St Malo the following morning was later than given due to the weather.

They set sail just after nine o'clock and hit heavy seas almost immediately. After a short browse through the various shops on board and a light snack in the self-service restaurant, she decided to go to bed and ride out the heavy seas in her sleep. Much to her relief, she soon fell asleep, dreaming about being on a roller coaster at the fairground.

She washed and dressed in the morning with more leisure than usual on such trips, knowing that there was no rush to get breakfast eaten before disembarking. In fact, she decided, she would have a full English breakfast instead of her usual continental one. Then, once she was on the road, she wouldn't need to stop for lunch.

She made her way to the restaurant, rolling along in a rhythm to match the pitch and toss of the seas. She was relieved to reach a table without falling over. Other passengers went through the same motions, laughing in good humour at their own antics. Every so often, the crash of cutlery or breakfast dishes announced the fall of a waiter's tray or some crockery falling off the edge of a table.

It was just after Giselle had finished her breakfast that an announcement over the public address system declared that their arrival in St Malo would be further delayed until four o'clock that afternoon since the overnight storm had blown the ferry off course and they were now limping their way back along the French coast in a northerly direction.

Her choice of breakfast no longer seemed a good idea. The only thing to do was to return to her cabin and lie down, hoping that the storm would calm down somewhat. She rose to her feet and steadied herself against the table before she set off across the dining area towards the doorway to the right. She had taken only four steps when the boat lurched sideways and she found herself being propelled in the opposite direction.

She lost her balance and flung out her arms towards a nearby pillar, and missed!

'Oh!' she cried out.

A strong hand caught hold of her elbow, steadying her. She looked up into a pair of dark blue eyes, as dark as the midnight sky, set in an olive-skinned face. The eyes were alight with laughter, crinkled at the corners. Giselle was mesmerised by them.

'Are you steady, now?'

The words were in perfect French, spoken by a voice that was deep but musical. Her eyes dropped to his lips. They were parted slightly, showing pure white teeth. A dimple at the lower edge of his left cheek deepened as she watched. She realised a question had been asked and floundered for a reply that would make sense because she couldn't for the life of her remember what the question had been!

Pull yourself together, girl! Stop looking like a fish gasping for air!

'Yes, thank you.'

She wasn't even sure if she had spoken in French or in English!

'I . . . er . . . ' she stammered.

'You fell into my arms.'

The young man smiled. He was still holding her elbow and had somehow drawn her much closer to him. Her body felt as though it was on fire. Her hands had risen to press against his chest and she could feel his steady heartbeat, much steadier than hers felt, that was for sure! She had no idea how long they had been standing together. Time seemed to have stood still.

She was acutely conscious that her reaction to the man's closeness was revealed by her dumbstruck expression and struggled to free herself.

'Thank you!' she said sharply, deliberately choosing to speak in English. 'You may release me, now. I have got my balance.'

'Would you like a cup of coffee with me?' the young man offered, smiling down at her.

He was well over six feet tall, she judged, tall for a Frenchman or maybe he just spoke the language well. She certainly wasn't going to ask!

'No, thank you. I have just breakfasted. I think I'll return to my cabin.'

'The sea is too rough for you?' he queried, in English, this time.

'Not at all! I . . . er . . . have a long drive ahead of me. I may as well rest whilst I can.'

He smiled widely, infuriatingly, Giselle thought.

'Maybe later, then? I'll look out for you!'

Not if I can help it, Giselle decided perversely. Her feelings were running amok and she wasn't sure she wanted this, not right now! She smiled faintly.

'Maybe!'

She knew he was watching her as she left the restaurant and tried to keep as steady as she could. As she went through the door, she couldn't help turning to glance over her shoulder. He was still there, and had the effrontery to raise a hand in a departing gesture! Giselle tilted back her head and turned away quickly. She shouldn't have looked!

The man stood still for a moment, the image of her face still imprinted on his mind. She was an attractive young woman and, for a moment, he wished she had accepted his offer of coffee. Then, with a shrug of his shoulders, he turned away. It was just as well she wasn't interested. The last thing he wanted right now was a romantic involvement!

The day passed slowly. Giselle read a few chapters of a book, slept a little, and ventured out for a late lunch round about two o'clock. She had a bowl of soup, a couple of small rolls of bread and a fruit salad. That should see her through the rest of the afternoon and, if she wanted anything later, there were plenty of service areas along the route where she could buy a baguette or a sandwich. There was no sign of the young Frenchman, for that's what she was sure he was. His dark hair and olive complexion pointed that way, though his English had been perfect.

By the time the boat had docked and unloaded, it was after five o'clock local time. A long, articulated lorry had jack-knifed across the main exit lane on the ferry, blocking the way. She realised that the tide would be at a different level from the one the lorry had been loaded for. The cars could cope with the steep descent and immediate rise, but the longer length of the lorry could not! They spent nearly an hour freeing it.

Giselle knew she now had two options. She could either book herself into a small hotel somewhere, or she could drive on regardless of the late hour and get to her destination after midnight. She chose the latter. At least she would be there, and she had had a good rest during the day.

Having made the decision, she quickly got on to her main road to lle D'Oleron. It was a straightforward journey, one that she knew well. Well before Bordeaux, she picked up on the La Rochelle signs on the auto-route. It was raining heavily by then and she only just caught sight of the sign as she peered through the swiftly-moving windscreen wipers. She immediately took the next exit and she slowed down on the ordinary roads. There wasn't much traffic. Not many were mad enough to be out on such an evening, she reflected wryly.

She always loved the approach to lle D'Oleron, but tonight, she was too tired to think about it. Not that she would have seen anything if she had tried. Visibility was minimal. The rain was hitting her windscreen horizontally and she was sure the viaduct was swaying in the wind. She was relieved to drive off it and be on her way round the sea marshes. This was the last stretch of her journey to Le Petit Village, a commune of Le Grand Village D'Oleron, which boasted one of the loveliest beaches on the island.

Le Petit Village was inland, situated on the edge of the marshes. The area was virtually uncrossable by anything other than watercraft, though some older islanders knew the ancient ways across them.

Giselle knew where the small cottage that her father had purchased was situated. It was just off the narrow road that ran through the small village. She felt she remembered it from her previous visits. He had said that you could see the restaurant, just across the narrow inlet at that point. Her eyebrows puckered as she tried to remember what was there but nothing came to mind. She was approaching the place right now but couldn't see anything at all through the downpour! That pleasure would have to wait until morning!

She parked her car at the side of the cottage and glanced at her watch. It was twenty-five past eleven. She was glad to have arrived before midnight. She would make a hot drink, she decided, and go straight to bed. Making sure she had the key to the cottage door handy, she leaped out of her car, grabbed her overnight bag off the rear seat and, slamming the car door shut with a swing of her hips, she ducked her head against the rain and ran up to the cottage door. It was glass-panelled and she could see that it was in total darkness inside.

Juggling with her bag, she managed to fit the key into the lock, but it wouldn't turn! Don't say she had brought the wrong key! That would just about be the finishing touch to a horrendous journey! She rattled the door handle and, to her surprise, the door swung open. It hadn't been locked! She shrugged off her initial wariness as there was so little crime on the island. She scooped up her bag and pushed her way into the main room of the cottage, pushing the door closed behind her with a thrust of her foot.

She bet she looked a sight! Her hair was hanging in wet strands around her face and rainwater was dripping down her neck. She dumped her bag and felt along the wall for a light switch. None was there! With a sinking of her spirit, she realised that there mightn't be any electricity connected! She was too tired to blunder around the room searching for whatever alternative form of lighting might exist.

It was a single-storey cottage, her father had said, having a living-room, a kitchen, a small bathroom and a bedroom. Please let there be blankets on the bed!

She stumbled back to the door and dropped the latch into place. Now, what had Dad said? The kitchen is to the left, the bedroom in the middle and bathroom to the right. The hot drink no longer held first place in her mental list of priorities. The bathroom held the first place, and bed held second and third places!

She had placed her leisure suit on the top of the clothes in her overnight bag and a towel to dry her hair was under that. She put down her bag and dragged the items out. The towel soon took the worst of the wetness off her hair and three minutes later she had pulled on her leisure suit, not caring if she put it on the right way round or not.

It was pitch black in the bedroom. Gingerly she felt her way forward.

'Ah!'

There it was! She felt her way along it. It certainly had some sort of cover on it, a duvet or sleeping-bag. That was good! Which end was the top? She inched her way along to the right. No, that was the foot. The other way, then. Yes! A pillow! She felt farther — and froze! Hair! A face! Then a hand grabbed her wrist, and she screamed!

# 3

'What do you think you are doing?' a masculine voice demanded in French, making Giselle see red.

What was she doing, indeed! She tried to pull free of the iron grip around her wrist, but couldn't!

'Never mind about me!' she declared sharply. 'Who are you? And what are you doing in my bed?'

Surprisingly, she had now lost the stab of fear that had initially shot through her. It was rage that was firing her.

'Your bed?' the masculine voice drawled. 'I think we might have to debate that question, young lady!'

Giselle yanked at her arm again, with no better result.

'You didn't answer my question!' she said coldly, unnerved by his calm assurance. 'Let go of my wrist and switch on some light. I presume you have got some light in here!'

In answer, the bright light of a flash lamp shone on her face, blinding her. As she recoiled from the effects of the light she heard the sharp sound of indrawn breath, followed by a low chuckle.

'Care for a cup of coffee?' the same drawled voice offered.

She bristled immediately.

'No, I wouldn't! At least, not until you have shown me your face and I know who you are!'

The glimmer of a suspicion began to seep into her mind, a suspicion that leaped into reality as the man turned the flash lamp on to his own face. It was the man from the ferry! Now, what on earth was he doing here?

'How . . . who are you? Who, first. How, afterwards!'

The man ignored her question. He released his hold on her wrist and, she sensed rather than saw, he began to get out of the bed.

'I'll turn on the lamp,' he offered calmly. 'Just a moment!'

She realised he was fumbling for matches and, within a moment or so, a lamp at the side of the bed flickered into life. He was holding out his hand towards her, but she refused to touch it.

'Jean Claude Morville,' the man said, his hand still outstretched. 'And you, no doubt, are Giselle Anderson.'

'So, you know me! Then you also know that my father owns this cottage. You still haven't told me what you are doing here!'

'It's rented, and he only rents half of it!' Jean Claude amended her statement of ownership.

'Half!'

She stepped backwards.

'What do you mean?'

Her brain was sifting through not only Jean Claude's words but also everything she could remember from the conversations she had had with her father before his accident.

'My father owns it all! He told me so.'

'Your father tried to buy it, but Madame Guillotine, next door, wouldn't sell, so he rented it. He borrowed half of the money for the restaurant and deposit on this place from my grandfather, Monsieur Thierry Morville,' Jean Claude patiently explained, as if he were talking to a child. 'When your father had the road traffic accident, my grandfather realised that he would probably lose his money, so, he is claiming his portion in the property and business venture!'

'I don't believe you!'

Jean Claude continued calmly, 'I am here to stake the claim on his behalf.'

'You can't do that!'

'I think you will find I can! Your father included such a clause in the loan agreement. I will show a copy to you in the morning. Didn't he show you his copy? It was all done legally, I assure you.'

Giselle bit her lip. She hadn't shown a great deal of interest in the purchase of the cottage and restaurant before the accident, and her father had not been in a position to tell her anything afterwards.

'My father is still in a coma,' she said with a catch in her voice. 'I just thought . . .'

'I'm sorry about that.'

His voice softened and he reached out to touch her arm. Although Giselle knew it was an act of compassion, she stepped away from him. She needed to keep her wits about her until she knew exactly what her position was regarding this man. In spite of his unnerving presence, she was aware of an inner feeling of intrigue about him. His manner was friendly. Still, that might be a ploy to throw her off her guard! She must remain detached from his undoubted charms.

'We were all greatly distressed when you wrote to tell us about your father,' Jean Claude was saying. 'Did you not receive our reply? I suppose not, or you would have known how things stand.'

He sounded genuinely upset, but Giselle didn't feel in the mood to meet him halfway. Her mind wanted to push the uncomfortable truth away and she found herself saying suspiciously, 'How is it I don't know you then? I used to visit your family quite often, but I don't remember you being around at any time.'

'My mother was my father's first wife. Their marriage didn't work out and they divorced, much to the disapproval of the rest of the family. I used to spend my holidays with my mother and her second husband in Marseilles, and, I suppose, no-one thought to mention the fact.'

'Why didn't you tell me who you were on the boat, instead of stringing me along like that?'

Her tone was still waspish, she knew, and she felt faintly ashamed of herself, but she wanted to cover all aspects, to be sure he was genuine. Jean Claude smiled disarmingly.

'I didn't know who you were. There

were any number of beautiful young ladies on board, and you did rather take me by surprise when you flung yourself into my arms! We might have discovered our relationship if you had accepted my offer of coffee,' he added teasingly.

Giselle ignored the latter part of his statement. She was remembering the feel of his arms about her, thankful that the lamp gave only a poor light. She knew her cheeks had reddened and she bet he knew how his closeness had melted her insides, the insufferable man!

'You were merely in the right place at the right time,' she said coolly. 'Anyone would have sufficed!'

'I was pleased to have been of service, and disappointed when you spurned my offer of coffee. But, no matter! We have plenty of time and opportunity to become acquainted now!'

Her eyes narrowed.

'What do you mean?'

'Simply that we shall be working together to build up the venture, of course! I don't intend to represent my father as a mere sleeping-partner!'

He emphasised the last two words, introducing an ambiguous meaning to them, his lopsided smile obviously meant to devastate her resistance!

'Yes! Well, we'll discuss that in the morning, shall we?' Giselle said briskly, determined not to let him see just how much he disturbed her, and she needed time to mull over the change of circumstances she now found herself to be in.

Just what rôle did he intend to take for himself — accounts manager, or something more hands on?

'I'll give the coffee a miss,' she decided. 'I'm tired and I would like to get to bed. That is . . . '

She hesitated, glancing around. Jean Claude had been in the only bed in the room.

'Don't worry! I won't lay claim to half the bed as well!' Jean Claude said, grinning at her discomfort. 'I have a sleeping bag. I'll sleep in the living-room, for tonight.'

He indicated his recently vacated bed.

'Be my guest!'

Giselle supposed she should have searched for fresh sheets but she was far too tired. With Jean Claude's revelations spinning through her mind, she didn't think she could fall asleep too readily, but she had no memory of lying awake when she opened her eyes the next morning. Jean Claude was standing by the bedside, a steaming cup of coffee in his hand.

'Bonjour! Your long-awaited coffee, mademoiselle!' he said with a smile. 'I have already set the fire in the stove, and the bathroom is free. Breakfast in twenty minutes. All right?'

'Er, bonjour. Thank you!' she added.

Once again she felt disadvantaged by him. Did he do it deliberately? She put the coffee on the small, bedside table and then swung her legs out of bed. She picked up the coffee again and took it over to the window. The storm had passed, though the sky remained overcast. The small, rear garden seemed unkempt. She pressed her face up against the windowpane and tried to look over to where she knew the marshes were, but the angle of the window was too sharp.

Her first view of the restaurant would have to wait until later. She had better drink up and follow Jean Claude into the bathroom. A partnership might have been forced upon her but she didn't intend to take a back seat or be forever trailing Jean Claude around! This was still her dad's project as far as she was concerned, and she was going to ensure it stayed that way!

Later, Giselle looked across the narrow strip of water, a puzzled expression on her face.

'Where is it?' she asked.

All she could see was a rickety, wooden bridge and a line of dilapidated wooden shacks standing on an equally dilapidated wooden quayside. Jean Claude looked down at her. His lips twitched as though he were trying hard to prevent a smile from lighting up his face. His dark eyes weren't so easily controlled and they danced with merriment.

'Where is what?' he asked, one eyebrow rising slightly, his expression giving away the fact that he was teasing her.

Giselle was in no mood to be amused.

'The restaurant, of course! What do you think?'

'It is there.'

He nodded towards the series of shacks, though his eyes never left her face. Giselle stared across at the cluster of huts, filled with dismay.

'It can't be,' she faltered. 'I know Dad said it was a failing business, but he didn't say that it had fallen down!'

'It isn't as bad as it looks. I have had it given a structural survey.'

His composure slipped for a moment, but he quickly recovered.

'The main foundations and supports are sound. Only one roof needs to be replaced. The others are damaged but can be repaired easily. The same with some of the walls. Most of the windows need to be replaced but that won't be a big job. As for the rest — a few coats of paint and creosote will work wonders!'

'It had better!'

'I will show you over it after breakfast. It won't seem so bad with a bit of food inside you. I don't suppose you ate much yesterday, did you? I know I never do when I'm driving down here. I always just want to arrive!'

Giselle warmed towards him. That was exactly how she always felt.

They ate croissants with honey drizzled over them and two cups of hot coffee, managing to chat a little about themselves and their favourite parts of the island, though, later, Giselle realised she still didn't know too much about Jean Claude's present circumstances. He hadn't mentioned a girl friend, she couldn't help thinking, surprised by the feeling of satisfaction that gave her. Had he manipulated the conversation towards her own details, or was she simply more chatty that he was?

As soon as breakfast was over, Giselle was keen to go over to inspect the buildings more closely. She still looked doubtfully at the wooden structure. No wonder she hadn't been able to imagine a restaurant on this site! She had probably ridden by the place countless times and taken no notice of the wooden shacks, thinking they were no more than fishermen's cabins, for that was exactly what they looked like!

Had her father really intended to restore them into a restaurant, or had he been conned by his wife's family into putting his money into something less viable?

Her father was a chef through and through. Business acumen hadn't been his strongest point.

Giselle looked hard at Jean Claude. He was busy poking at some of the wooden walls where anybody with half an eye could see daylight showing through! He had a survey, indeed! By whom and was he qualified?

'What did you say your job was, Jean Claude?' she asked him lightly.

'Er . . .'

He hesitated and straightened up.

'I'm a . . . er . . . general dogsbody at the moment. You know, jack of all trades.'

'And master of none!' she finished tartly.

She narrowed her eyes as she faced him squarely. He didn't strike her as being somebody to be satisfied with an unqualified career. So, what was his motive?

'What's in it for you, getting my father to put his money into a heap of rubbish?'

'It isn't a heap of rubbish,' he replied quietly. 'A qualified surveyor did the survey, and it's mostly sound! Look, we've put some of our money into it as well! Equal parts! I told you! That's why I'm here! We want to see some return on it and . . . '

'So, who did it? One of your buddies?'

'Does it matter who did it? My father trusts him, and my grandfather. Look, let's get a local builder in and see what he says. He can give us an estimate, and we can take it from there.'

'Is he another of your buddies?'

'I know him. He's a good worker.'

'He'll need to be! Look, I'll pick someone, as well. Then we can compare their estimates. In fact, I'll pick two, unknowns, to compare with your henchman! How's that?'

She stood watching him, hands on her hips, taping her foot. Jean Claude laughed.

'You drive a hard bargain, for a little one! Agreed?'

What had she to lose?

'All right. I agree, as long as I get to choose which one!'

'It's a deal!'

They continued inspecting the structures, in a more congenial manner.

Giselle had to admit that Jean Claude seemed to know what he was talking about. Had she judged him too harshly? She didn't know, and, besides, even if the survey was genuine, there was no harm in checking. Better safe than sorry!

The first two shacks had been used as stores. There were some boxes of foodstuffs stacked in one, but all out of date. They'd have to get rid of all those. The other one held a freezer that looked as if it could be in working order. At least it meant that electricity had been installed here!

'Why is there no electricity in our part of the cottage?' she asked.

'It was just part of Madame Tessier's house, a sort of storage area. She lives in the other two thirds of the building.'

'Is she another buddy, or member of your family?'

'No! I disown her completely! She's an old martinet! Just you wait until you meet her. You'll see what I mean!'

'Sounds interesting! Can we put in

electricity? It would make life a lot easier. I'm not too good with oil lamps and such.'

'Madame Tessier wasn't very co-operative on that matter. She says we must wait until we know how long we want to rent the place. She doesn't want to pay for something that might not get used very much.'

'I suppose that's understandable. Would it cost a lot?'

'Ian said he'll see to it, that is, if we choose his estimate! He won't over-charge for it.'

'Ian?'

'My buddy, as you like to call him. He's a bit of an ex-patriot of yours really. Came over here about ten years ago and has built up quite a good business. He's well known for his fairness and reliability,' he added smoothly, casting a lopsided grin at her.

'Hmm! If you say so! Now, then, let's get on with the rest of the buildings, shall we?'

The next two shacks had been

converted into one. The first portion was the kitchen, containing much-used but neglected ovens and hobs. Everything needed a good clean and sorting out, but she reckoned they had been good implements in their time. There were quite a number of cupboards and work-tops and she was beginning to see what her father had probably seen in the place. It did have potential, eventually!

Through the serving-hatch, she could see the seating area and she made for the connecting door. It was the swing-type, so that the waiter or waitress would only need to push against it to open it, a must in a busy kitchen! At first she grimaced. Everywhere was filthy. The tables had old Formica tops, much stained and chipped. The chairs looked none too stable and the wooden floor had holes right through to the salt-water that lay beneath.

'We need a new floor in here,' Jean Claude said, before she could speak. 'Tread carefully! That will be one of the first jobs to be done, and out here.'

He led the way to the outer door. There was no furniture out there, but Giselle could see, in her mind's eye, a gaily-decorated terrace, partly under cover, partly in the open.

'We could have tables with brightly-coloured parasols,' she suggested, her eyes lighting with enthusiasm. 'We'd get, let's see, about eight or ten tables out here, maybe six under the veranda cover, and eight or ten inside, say, between twenty-two to twenty-four tables. That's about fifty to eighty covers per night. What d'you think?'

Jean Claude was watching her with an amused smile on his face.

'We'll have to build it up slowly,' he warned, 'but, yes, I think that number could eventually be catered for. Don't forget, there will only be the two of us, at first, so let's not be too ambitious to start with.'

Giselle looked at him in surprise.

'The two of us?' she queried. 'Do you intend working here, too, once it's up and running, I mean?'

Jean Claude raised his eyebrows slightly and gave an almost imperceptible nod.

'Of course! I have to protect our investment, don't I? And, why pay another wage when I can do the job myself?'

# 4

Giselle cast him a querying look then asked, 'And just which job do you see yourself doing, Jack-of-all-trades?'

Jean Claude laughed.

'Don't worry! I'm not about to steal yours! I can do a bit of cooking but I know my limits! No, I'll be Ian's labourer, should you choose his estimate, and the handsome waiter, once we are up and running! Does that suit you, mademoiselle?'

Giselle found herself blushing somewhat. He certainly knew he was good-looking, and he was quite agreeable to get on with! She hadn't even considered that they would be actually working together so closely, but she supposed he was as good as anybody else. She wouldn't be able to manage on her own, that was for sure, and his presence made the renovation work seem more feasible. In fact, the thought that she might have been faced with the enormity of it all on her own made her shudder inwardly. She didn't think she could have faced it!

She shrugged slightly, trying to convey a casual air.

'I suppose so, as long as we don't get under each other's feet. Where do you live, by the way?'

Jean Claude grinned and nodded back across the marshes.

'Didn't I tell you? I live in that desirable little cottage, across the way!'

Giselle was aware that her mouth was opening and closing like a fish, but no sound was coming out. She had thought his staying the previous night was due to his late hour of arrival. He had already explained to her that he had disembarked quite early, well before the incident with the articulated lorry, and had arrived at about ten o'clock, but she had imagined that he had stayed over in order to meet her this morning, not because it was where he intended to live.

She had been going to say that it was too small, but it wasn't the size that bothered her! It was the lack of privacy! The one bedroom! Jean Claude was watching her, she realised. His annoying habit of raising one eyebrow in silent query made her feel quite defensive.

'There's only one bed!' she snapped, 'and I don't intend sharing it!'

'We could take night about,' he suggested calmly, 'which makes it your turn on the lumpy sofa tonight!'

She glared at him, unsure whether or not he was joking. She was afraid that he wasn't! She liked her creature comforts too much to relish lying on the sofa every other night.

'Can't you live at home, with your father, I mean? I seem to remember there were plenty of bedrooms, whenever we went to stay.'

'Ah!' he shrugged. 'It's my half-sister, Christine. You remember her, do you?'

'Yes.'

'She and Henri and their two children are staying there at the moment. They are between houses. Besides, I don't feel it would be too wise for you to live here alone, with only an elderly neighbour for protection.'

'Nonsense! You know as well as I do that there's a very low crime rate on the island! There are all those cottages opposite, as well, and some more just down the lane. I'd be well looked after! In any case,' she added, 'I can take good care of myself!'

'I'm sure you can, but there are other reasons!'

'Oh, yes? Such as?'

'Number one, finances! When your father costed everything out, he realised that he would have to live as cheaply as possible until everything was up and running. That's why he rented a cottage instead of buying one. He intended to live in one of the cabins once one was habitable, which would save money again.'

That sounded reasonable, she supposed.

'And number two?'

Jean Claude had the grace to look slightly shame-faced.

'I'm not too good at getting up early, I'm afraid. So, I want to live on the job, so to speak. There's a great deal to be done and, once we start, we'll need to be up as soon as it's light and work through until dusk! That's if you want us to be ready for the start of the season, which, I presume, you do!'

'When does the season start around here?'

'The main season is July and August. You know what it's like then. The island almost capsizes, there are so many visitors! But, if we want to start early and work our way into it gradually, there will be visitors around from early May, especially for the various fête days and weekends, and June is getting to be a popular month as well, which only gives us, let me see, three weeks in March and four weeks in April. Seven weeks altogether!'

Giselle gaped at him.

'Seven weeks! You must be crazy! We'll never be ready in seven weeks!'

'We will if Ian starts straight away! He'll work round the clock for his food and lodgings!'

Giselle considered his words. It made sense, but it took away her initiative of having some say in the matter of whom to employ. Was it worth making a stand? She decided it wasn't! There wasn't enough time. She pressed her lips together. He had known that, when he had agreed to let her get two estimates! For a moment, she felt a wave of rebellion rising within her, but she fought against it. All it would achieve was a tighter schedule for the much-needed repairs.

'All right,' she conceded ungraciously, 'but I'll want to see every bill that we pay and verify every transaction!'

'But, of course!'

He grinned triumphantly as he

looked at his watch.

'He'll be here at two o'clock this afternoon, which just gives us time to decide what cleaning materials we need to buy.'

Giselle was furious.

'You've already engaged him, haven't you? You had no intention of letting me get other estimates!'

Jean Claude smiled appeasingly.

'You would have chosen Ian, anyway! He has a good reputation and asks a reasonable price. Ask around if you wish. You'll find that I'm right! You'll get on with him. He's a great guy!'

Giselle scowled, prepared to hate him on sight.

'Where will he stay?' she asked suspiciously, suddenly sensing that their limited accommodation was about to shrink even more.

Jean Claude spread his hands.

'We could pay for him to take lodgings somewhere but it would cost quite a bit! As I said, he'll be out working most of the time. All he needs is a bed, and mountains of food, and you'll be good at providing that! It will be good practice for you!'

Giselle sighed in defeat.

'You win! I suppose he'll act as a chaperon for us! Safety in numbers and all that!'

She couldn't help feeling that she had been led by her nose, but, under the circumstances, she felt she had no option but to go along with Jean Claude's plan and hope that he was as committed as she was to getting the best man and materials at the best possible price. She realised that things would be pretty tight for a while but a sense of excitement was swelling deep within her. Her dad had had a vision for the place, and, now, so had she!

There was just one more cabin to view, right at the end of the wooden pier.

'What about that one?' Giselle asked, nodding across to it.

Jean Claude followed her gaze.

'That one holds some fishing gear

and the rakes and baskets the salt-collectors used. Did you ever see them in action, when the salt-beds were in use?'

Giselle nodded.

'Yes. I came round here once or twice. I used to wonder what the little white piles were and, one summer, an old man took us round the salt-beds and told us how he let in the sea water, then dammed the outlet and waited for the sun to evaporate the water away. He let us rake some of it to the side for him. When we came back the following year, he wasn't here. We made a few salt piles ourselves, but it rained the next day and washed it all away!'

'That would be old Pierre. He died, and everything fell into disrepair. Victor Perrotin ran the restaurant for a few more seasons, but it became too much for him. He was glad to get a buyer for the property and a bit extra for goodwill.'

He placed a hand on Giselle's shoulder and turned her to face towards the road that ran through the village.

'His cousin, Denis, still owns those other large huts by the roadside. He sells local wines and other local products from one of them and is planning to develop the other two into a living museum. When we have got the restaurant up and running, I'm thinking of seeing if we can join forces and develop the salt-beds again. A lot of birds live in these marshes. I'm mulling over the possibility of developing a sort of bird sanctuary, opening up the waterways and placing hides at strategic points.'

He was staring out over the overgrown salt-beds with a faraway look in his eyes, as if he were seeing the eventual outcome of his thoughts.

'I think people will be interested, don't you? And it will bring customers to the restaurant and Denis's wine cave.'

Giselle looked at him with renewed respect. He wasn't just intending to disappear from the scene, then, when the restaurant was launched. She felt a warming deep within her and, when he turned to catch her reaction to his words, the depth of her feelings towards him unexpectedly confused her.

'That sounds great,' she stammered, caught unawares.

His eyes crinkled at the corners and his mouth looked extremely kissable, she couldn't help thinking, but she needed to keep a clear head for the success of her father's venture, and that didn't include romantic involvement. So she pushed the thoughts aside and smiled brightly.

'Well, if that's all, we had better get on with things or the morning will be gone before we've done everything we need to see us through the day.'

After making a phone call to the hospital back home and discovering that there was no change in her father's condition, they did their shopping, returning with a car full of boxes, bags and packets of cleaning materials from the local hardware store.

They had also popped into the local supermarket, and bought a selection of basic foodstuffs and, whilst Giselle had been seeing to that, Jean Claude had bought two serviceable camp beds for himself and Ian and another sleeping bag.

The source of cooking in the cottage was bottled gas, as was their main lighting, Giselle discovered. A limited amount of cooking implements was available and an odd assortment of crockery and cutlery. However, they decided to make do with what they had, for the time being, and concentrate on fitting up the kitchen in the restaurant. Once that was established, she would be able to cook their meals over there, so it seemed a bit unnecessary to buy for the cottage. If Jean Claude had made an accurate assessment, they wouldn't be spending much time in the cottage anyway.

After a lunch of fish soup and a wonderfully fresh baguette, they were joined by Ian. Giselle had to concede reluctantly that Jean Claude's estimation of him was correct. He was a nice guy and was easy to get on with. She soon found out that he was married and lived on the mainland, with his wife and small family, who were visiting relations in England for a few weeks, hence his willingness to live-in and work round the clock.

The two men wanted to get started straightaway, concentrating on making the buildings structurally sound and weatherproofed.

'We'll clear all the rubbish out this afternoon,' Ian decided. 'I'll get hold of a skip from somewhere. The forecast is quite good for the next few days. If we can get the roofs done while it's dry, we'll be able to work on in any weather until the outside painting needs doing. How does that sound?'

His question was directed at Giselle.

'Fine!' she replied, sensing his reliability instantly.

She avoided catching Jean Claude's

eye. He was standing behind Ian looking rather smug, she thought rebelliously. She tossed her hair over her shoulder and swung around on her heels.

'I'll leave you two boys to it then. Give me a shout if you need an extra hand for anything!'

Giselle began in the kitchen. There was a lot of sorting out to do before she could get to grips with the cooking range and cleaning attack on every inch of the place. She knew there would be a health inspection before she could open for business and didn't intend to be turned down through infringing any local bylaws regarding health and safety.

It was getting dark by the time she decided to finish for the day and she still had to prepare something for supper for the three of them. She thought longingly of the menus she intended to create once the restaurant was ready, but none of that for tonight. She had willingly cheated and bought two large packs of frozen paella from the supermarket! With a fresh green salad and two baguettes, it would be a feast fit for kings!

'Give me half an hour,' she called to the men. 'I need a wash and then I'll get supper ready! Don't work too long. It's getting too dark to see!'

She managed to light the gas lamps and decided to strip off for a wash in the bathroom. She realised that hot water must be piped in from next door, much to her relief. A cold shower wasn't her favourite penance!

As she stepped out of the shower, the sound of banging on the communal wall with the next cottage drew her attention. She could hear the old lady's voice shouting something but couldn't make out the words. She knocked back, to indicate that she had heard and wrapped a large towel around herself. The banging was now on the cottage door.

'One moment!' she called out, looking for something more substantial to wear before she opened the door.

The banging continued. Exasperated, Giselle opened the door, more conscious of the icy wind than her dishevelled appearance.

'Yes? Is something the matter?' she enquired, speaking more sharply than she had intended.

An elderly woman stood there, wrapped in a large coat and a shawl over her head.

'I want no more banging of doors in the middle of the night like last night!' she rasped in French as soon as the door opened. 'You are a woman! Monsieur Anderson said nothing of a woman living here! And you have no clothes on! Have you no shame, mademoiselle?'

Giselle felt her face redden.

'I have just had a shower!' she tried to explain.

The woman didn't even pause.

'I want none of your loose city ways in my house! I'll not have it, d  vou hear!'

She shook her clenched fist in Giselle's face. Giselle involuntarily took a step backwards. No wonder Jean Claude had called her Madame Guillotine! However, it wouldn't do to start off on the wrong foot with her. She cleared her throat and tried again.

'I'm sorry, Madame. It was my father who rented the cottage from you, but he has been in a car accident and is still unconscious. I have come to get his business up and running, with Monsieur Morville, of course!'

The old woman's face softened for a fleeting second.

'I am sorry about your father, Mademoiselle Anderson, but I won't have scandalous goings-on in my cottage! Either one of you goes, or, at the end of the month I will foreclose your tenancy agreement! Is that clear?'

# 5

Giselle stared at her in dismay, and tried her best to explain the situation in the cottage.

'There is nothing immoral going on,' she protested. 'We are merely sharing the cottage to save on money. The two men will be sleeping in the living-room.'

'Two men!'

The woman's eyes nearly popped out her head.

'Non! Non! Non! I will not have it!'

'We have paid the rent!' Giselle insisted.

'But it is my cottage! I will be living here long after you have moved on, as you young people do! I have my reputation to think of!'

The two women glared at each other, neither intending to back down. It was Giselle who brought the confrontation to a close.

'You must excuse me, madame. I need to get dressed and cook our supper. Jean Claude will come to see you later.'

Jean Claude took the news calmly when she told him.

'We have done nothing to merit an eviction and we have paid a month's rent.'

He smiled reassuringly, reaching out to playfully tickle her under her chin.

'Don't worry about it. I will go round later on and turn my irresistible charm on to her.'

His hand stilled and his smile faded. His face took on a serious air. Giselle caught her breath as their eyes met. He was standing very close. She could feel her heart thumping rapidly. He cupped her chin in his hand and gently tilted it towards his face. As he began to lower his head towards her, she saw a movement at the window. It wasn't quite dark out there and she could see the lined face of Madame Tessier peering into the room, her hands cupped around her eyes.

'She's out there, watching us!' Giselle hissed, trying to pull away.

Jean Claude held her chin firmly, though not hurting her. He placed his other hand in the small of her back and drew her forward.

'Then, let's give her something to see!' he suggested.

His mouth covered hers gently, his lips feeling smooth and warm. After an initial moment of protest, Giselle began to respond. She forgot the face at the window and opened herself to the kiss. It felt wonderful. She wanted it to go on and on. The steady beat of his heart seemed to regulate the beat of her own, so that they beat in unison.

Somehow, her hands had risen and were around his neck, her fingers sliding into his short dark hair. She was aware of every contour of his lithe body pressing against her. She had the wild thought that he might sweep her up into his arms and . . .

A loud rapping at the window broke

into their consciousness and both pulled apart. Giselle was shaken by the intensity of the kiss, and by her reacting to it. Jean Claude stirred more emotions within her than Daniel had ever done. Her fingers rose involuntarily and lightly touched her lips, trying to capture the now fading sensation.

Jean Claude felt shaken, too. He shouldn't have kissed her! It was asking for trouble! Hadn't he already decided that there was no room for romance this summer, not until everything was sorted out? It wouldn't be fair, on either of them! He forced his mouth into a humorous smile.

'Well, that should give her something to think about!' he said wryly, as Madame Tessier rapped loudly on the window again.

He looked down at Giselle, feeling guilty at the hurt look on her face but was unable to think of anything to say that wouldn't make the situation even more awkward. Instead, he sighed.

'I'd better go and speak to her before

she breaks the window and claims our deposit in recompense.'

He let go of Giselle and strode to the door. She felt as though her face had been slapped. Was that what the kiss had been about, just a mischievous gesture to annoy their landlady? Her fingers were against her cheeks, feeling the red-hot heat of them. Her breath caught in her throat.

She turned quickly and went into the tiny kitchen, thankful that she hadn't said anything to indicate what the kiss had meant to her. She felt a complete idiot. She mustn't let him know how she had felt! The paella was practically ready and she busied herself cutting some of the bread and putting a bowl of salad on to the table, thankful to have something to occupy herself. When she heard the door opening again, she was relieved to see that Ian was coming in with Jean Claude, both laughing.

'What did she say?' Giselle asked, trying to pretend that the kiss had never happened.

'We are part of a licentious generation and she is not having any of that in her house!' Jean Claude quoted, putting the same inflections into his voice that Giselle could well imagine Madame Tessier having used.

'What shall we do?'

'We've got nearly three weeks before she can evict us. Let's eat first and then we'll see how long we think the work will take.'

The paella was tasty, even though it was from the freezer, and the wonderful French bread quickly disappeared. After supper they discussed their work so far and Ian made a tentative plan for their procedure. They brainstormed it from all angles and eventually felt satisfied that, given a run of good weather and no untoward complications, they could make one of the huts habitable by the end of the month and complete the rest of the repairs well within their time limit up to the start of the season.

Giselle was glad when the two men

decided that they had done enough business talk for one day and, pleading the need for an early night, she left them together in the living-room with a few cans of beer. She didn't sleep readily. Her body had been awakened by Jean Claude's kiss and she could still feel the tingling of her lips as she relived it in her mind. Daniel's kisses had never made her feel like that, nor had any other of her boyfriends. But she didn't want this! It made life too complicated!

Her last thought before drifting into a restless sleep was that, apparently, neither did Jean Claude. This kiss had meant nothing to him, apart from winding up Madame Tessier. All she had to do was play it cool, and to pretend that it had meant nothing to her!

The next couple of weeks passed quickly. She was happy to renew her acquaintance with other members of Jean Claude's family. Christine had always been friendly and promised to help out at busy times if she was able to get someone to look after her children. Uncle Thierry looked a lot older than when she had last seen him and he was obviously glad to have relinquished his part of the business in Jean Claude's hands. They all expressed their sorrow at her dad's accident and wished him a speedy recovery.

Giselle still telephoned the hospital nearly every other day but, so far, there was no change in his condition. Still, it was early days yet and Giselle wouldn't let herself become too morbid about the possibility of him not recovering at all. She took time to record a tape about all that was happening at the restaurant and sent it to the hospital for someone to play to her dad. It might penetrate through into his subconscious mind. She had heard that such things were sometimes successful.

There were a few days of dry weather, long enough to complete the roof repairs and strengthen the wooden pier. The new wood was already seasoned and soaked in wood-preservative and the addition of the green and blue undercoating to some of the huts made the dream something of a reality. By the time the rain returned, Jean Claude and Ian had already started on internal work. Ian repaired what was necessary in the kitchen and Jean Claude worked alone in the dining area of the restaurant.

Giselle wondered if that had been Jean Claude's decision but nothing in his manner hinted at any estrangement between them. Giselle began to wonder if she had over-reacted to his remark after their kiss, though he made no move to renew any intimacy. She kept herself busy in the kitchen. The cooking range came up a treat with a vigorous rubdown and black-leading. The tiled walls and floor cleaned up better than she had hoped and the new, lightly-coloured worktops gave the whole place an attractive, hygienic appearance.

She scrubbed out the cupboards, repainted them in white and lined the shelves. A few days touring the wholesale suppliers of kitchen equipment enabled her to order the equipment they needed and she stood back in satisfaction when it was installed into place less than a week later. By then, the two men had started on the inner walls of the storerooms, making a complete inner lining and by the time the end of the month came, they declared it snug and warm enough to sleep in, leaving Giselle on her own in the cottage.

They still came over for showers but their gesture persuaded Madame Tessier that there were no immoral goings-on in her property and Giselle hoped that Madame Tessier's nightly banging on the communal wall would become a thing of the past.

Leaving Jean Claude and Ian to continue with the structural work, Giselle turned her attention to the catering side of the business. That was what she was here to do and she was longing to make a start. She had decided to make it a completely fish and seafood restaurant. There were plenty of other restaurants where meat was served and she didn't want theirs to be a mere replica of other establishments.

Her first task was to get to know the local fishermen and discover the best places to buy her fresh fish on a daily basis. She told the fishermen of her project and she was well received as a potential buyer. She loved the fresh smell of the sea and the raucous cry of the seagulls as they wheeled and swooped over the large baskets of the night's catch. Any faint question in her mind of what she might have been doing in Paris were no more than casual thoughts. Her father had been right. This was where she belonged.

'Why don't you come to the port with me?' she invited Jean Claude one day.

Most of the structural work was now finished and Ian had gone to do a few days' servicing of gas boilers at a nearby park of mobile homes.

'We'll buy some bread on our way back and have some fresh fish for breakfast. There's nothing like it!'

He groaned at the mention of the early hour he would have to rise but he made it and was ready in his thick sweater and jeans when she tooted her horn at six o'clock the following morning.

'It's the best time to buy fish,' she told him. 'Our sense of taste and smell is keener in the mornings.'

There were sardines of various sizes, herrings, mackerel, red mullet and red snappers, sea bass, cod, perch and skate. He watched as she touched the flesh of each fish to see how firm it was, turning back the fin, choosing those that were stiff, with red or pink gills and bright eyes.

'If the eyes are dull, it was probably part of yesterday's catch and best thrown back for the gulls to snatch at!' she said over her shoulder.

The fishermen soon learned that she

knew her stuff and respected her for it.

'I only want the best,' she told them. 'I'll pay a fair price, but don't think I'll pay above the odds! I'll be keeping an eye on everyone else's prices, too!'

There was a huge choice of crustaceans, all stored in large crates or wicker baskets — crabs, lobsters, langoustines and the smaller prawns. All kinds of shellfish abounded — cockles, mussels, clams and scallops and, her favourites, oysters galore!

She bought in small quantities, enough to feed the three of them, trying out recipes both old and new, filling the newly-renovated kitchen with delicious smells, enough to tempt the faintest of appetites — let alone the hale and hearty ones of her hard-working companions!

'I shan't want to leave!' Ian joked one day, as he tucked into Oyster Chowder.

The work was nearly completed now and the end of April was drawing near. The new tables they had ordered had been delivered and just needed to be set into place. Brightly-coloured parasols were ready for sunny days and the indoor décor of fishing nets and other fishing regalia needed to be positioned around the dining area and the final coats of blue and green paint on the outside of two of the cabins had to be done. They were nearly there!

'Better not let your wife hear that!' Giselle rejoined. 'I tell you what you must do! When we are open for business and Jill is back from England, you must come over for a proper meal. I'm hoping to have a special launching, too, with wine and finger foods. Consider yourself invited!'

Visitors were beginning to come to the island, especially at the weekends. They weren't quite ready to open for the bank holiday at the beginning of May but Giselle set her sights on being fully operational by the last weekend in May, on the French Mother's Day.

The dreaded day of the inspection by the ministry of health and hygiene came. Giselle hovered behind the representative as he peered and poked and took swabs from the various work surfaces. His face was inscrutable as he worked but he managed a faint smile at the end of his visit.

'It all seems fine, Mademoiselle Anderson, but you will have my official report in about a week's time. Don't cook anything for anyone other than yourself in the meantime.'

'You need a break,' Jean Claude said to her that afternoon.

Why not! There was nothing she could do until she received the all-clear from the inspection.

They decided to pack some fruit and bottles of water into Jean Claude's car and crossed to the Atlantic side of the island to Le Grand Village Plage. Jean Claude had borrowed two body-boards and they spent an exhilarating hour riding the waves that pounded upon the coast at the side of the island, waves so powerful that they were swept up on to the sandy beach time after time.

'That was great!' Giselle said, as she

flung herself on to her towel on the dry, powdery sand at the top of the beach.

The sun was hot, even though it was only early May.

'I'll put some sun-cream on your back,' Jean Claude offered. 'You have been inside too much during the last few weeks.'

His skin was already beginning to tan, since he had worn only shorts on some days. Giselle steeled herself not to be affected by his touch as he spread the cream across her back, but it was hard to remain distanced from it.

'Roll over!' he commanded.

She did so, but held out her hand for the sun cream.

'I can do my front,' she said as casually as she could, but he held the bottle out of her reach.

'What are you afraid of?'

'Nothing! Why should I be?'

'Are you afraid I will kiss you?'

'No.'

To be quite honest, she longed for him to kiss her again, even though it had meant nothing to him.

'I . . . er . . . quite enjoyed your kiss,' she admitted hesitantly. 'Not that it meant anything, of course!' she added hastily.

'Of course not! Friends can kiss without it being a big deal!'

He squirted a small amount of cream on to his hands and began to apply it gently to her upper chest. She tried to look away but she knew that he was watching her, his eyes glimmering with amusement.

'What's so funny?' she demanded.

'You are! You are dying for me to kiss you again.'

'No, I'm not!' she lied, and ran the moist tip of her tongue over her lips, full of longing to have his lips on hers. 'I don't want a serious romantic involvement!'

Jean Claude's eyebrows rose.

'Who said anything about being serious? If we are of the same mind, there is no reason why we cannot be friends, is there? Kissing friends, I mean!'

Her breath caught in her throat. Jean Claude was grinning infuriatingly at her, his mouth now only inches above hers.

'You're going to have to ask me to kiss you, or else I won't,' he teased.

She considered pushing him away, but her body longed for his touch. She relaxed back against the sand, mesmerised by the glint in his eyes and the tantalising curve of his mouth, coming closer and closer.

'Kiss me!' she whispered, unable to resist.

She sighed deeply as his lips covered hers. She revelled in the intimacy. Just as she was beginning to wonder what their next move would be, Jean Claude rolled off her, still holding on to her shoulders. Over and over they rolled in the sand, laughing wildly with the fun of their action.

When they came to rest, Jean Claude was gazing down at her. His eyes were still laughing but his face had sombred somewhat.

'Did that mean anything?' he asked softly.

Giselle lay still for a moment. The whole world had shaken, but she wasn't going to admit to that! She forced a grin.

'It was nice,' she said, as if after great consideration.

'Nice!' Jean Claude exclaimed. 'I must be losing my touch! We had better have some daily practice! What do you say, eh?'

Giselle grinned again.

'That's fine by me! But I'm covered in sand now and I'm going back in for a swim to wash it off!'

She heaved him away and ran back into the sea, followed closely by Jean Claude. They splashed and swam for another half-hour, had lunch, and then dug for clams in the sand, filling the plastic bag that had held their fruit.

'I'll make soup with those, for our dinner,' she promised, happy at the way their relationship was now going.

She wasn't sure what Jean Claude

expected from it, if anything, and there was no reason for him to know just how much he was beginning to mean to her. If nothing came of it by the end of the season, no harm would have been done, though a small voice in the depths of her heart disagreed with that last thought.

A week later, the promised report came from the health inspector. Despite knowing that everything was as hygienic as it could possibly be, she couldn't help feeling nervous as she ripped open the envelope. Her eyes skimmed over the report, anxious to read the final statement. A delighted grin lit her face.

'We've done it!' she called out to Jean Claude.

'What's that?'

'The health and hygiene report! We've passed!'

He came and stood behind her, his hands looped about her waist as he read the report over her shoulder.

'I knew there'd be no risk of failure, but, well done, all the same! This calls for a celebration! Come on! Drop all work! We'll go out to lunch somewhere! It will be our last opportunity before we open.'

They went to St Trojan and had a light lunch in a restaurant at the port, followed by a stroll hand in hand along the quayside.

Jean Claude had been right about it being their last opportunity for some relaxation. They had decided to have the launch the second Wednesday in May. Jean Claude contacted a friend in the printing trade who ran off a few thousand leaflets and they spent a wild weekend flooding the island with them, handing them out in the town centres, with the help of Jean Claude's niece and nephew, and posting them on lamp-posts, hoardings and along the sea fronts.

Giselle made what seemed like thousands of canapés, freezing what she could and working all the hours of the days leading up to the opening day. She invited Madame Tessier, but the grumpy old woman shut the door in her face.

'Your loss, not mine!' Giselle said to the closed door, pulling a wry face.

She wasn't used to living with bad feelings between neighbours, but there was nothing she could do about it, it seemed.

The launch was a huge success. People drifted in and out all afternoon, including Jean Claude's family and Ian and his wife. They were suitably impressed with the way things were looking and were lavish with their praise. Giselle was pleased that they were so happy with everything. The only person missing was her father!

A friendly reporter put a large spread about it in the local paper and a number of advance bookings were made for Mother's Day. She returned to the cottage mid-evening, intending to have a shower and go out somewhere on the island for a relaxing drink with Jean Claude, and have a meal maybe as she had eaten very little during the afternoon.

As she slipped out of her dress, she heard banging on the internal wall. She sighed with exasperation. What now? Surely there was nothing Madame Tessier could complain about? If she hadn't liked all the comings and going of cars and people, it was her own lookout! She had had her invitation and refused it!

The banging started again. Giselle froze for a moment, the truth suddenly hitting her! There had been no cause for annoyance — the bangs were a call for help! She pulled her dress back over her head and hurried outside. The sun had long set and the evening was drawing in but there was no light on in the room, even though Giselle knew that electricity was laid on in the larger cottage.

She held her face to the window next door and peered through the glass. Madame Tessier was lying on the floor.

# 6

Giselle hesitated. She wished Jean Claude had come back with her. Should she waste time running for him? Another look through the window persuaded her to try to gain entry, if only to reassure Madame Tessier that help was at hand.

She ran round to the back and was relieved to find a door open. She hadn't been inside the cottage before, but she pushed open the door and made her way inside.

'I'm coming, Madame Tessier!' she called out, making her way to the darkened front room.

'I'm in here!'

'Yes, I know. I saw you through the window.'

She dropped down at Madame Tessier's side, barely able to see her.

'What has happened?'

'I think I've broken my leg,' Madame

Tessier gasped painfully. 'I can't move it. My back hurts, too.'

'I'll switch the light on, shall I?'

Giselle rose to her feet.

'There's no bulb in,' Madame Tessier said in short gasps. 'That's what I was doing.'

Giselle almost fell over what she realised was a fallen stool. She steadied herself.

'Is there a light in the kitchen?'

'Yes, just by the door. Go carefully.'

Giselle felt her way around the furniture, marvelling that she had missed it all on her way in. She located the light switch and turned it on. Then she returned to the front room, now able to make out where Madame Tessier lay. She could see at a glance that her leg was twisted under her at a funny angle.

'I don't think I should move you,' Giselle murmured, as much to herself as to the elderly woman. 'I need to get help. Where's your telephone, madame?'

'I haven't got one.'

'Oh! Then I'm going to have to leave you for a moment or two. Don't worry! I'll be right back.'

She ran across the road, over the bridge and burst into the cabin where Jean Claude was putting the finishing touches to his casual evening clothes. He looked up in surprise, even more so as he took in her dishevelled appearance.

'What's wrong?'

Giselle didn't hesitate.

'It's Madame Tessier. She's fallen! I think she's broken her leg. Will you ring for an ambulance?'

'Good heavens! Yes, of course!'

He quickly took out his mobile phone and dialled the emergency number and gave the necessary information to the operator.

'Right! Let's get back to her and see what we can do to make her comfortable.'

They hurried back together, Giselle almost running to keep up with Jean Claude's long strides. She was relieved to be sharing the responsibility with him. She only had a smattering of first aid knowledge and didn't want to make anything worse for the elderly woman. Jean Claude agreed with her assessment of the injuries.

'Go to her bedroom and bring a blanket to cover her,' he told Giselle.

He reach for a slim cushion on the sofa and placed it carefully under her head.

'Try to relax, Madame Tessier,' he said calmly.

When Giselle returned with a blanket, he was rubbing Madame Tessier's hands, trying to bring some warmth back into them. Giselle carefully wrapped the blanket over her, tucking it under her uninjured side.

'What were you doing, trying to change the bulb?' she asked. 'You shouldn't be climbing on to stools at your age!'

'You might think I'm old but I'm not finished yet!' Madame Tessier retorted spiritedly. 'I've always looked after myself, and I always will!'

'Yes. I'm sorry I implied you are too old. I didn't mean it like that, but you really shouldn't be climbing up on stools. Why didn't you ask one of us to fix it for you? We would have done, you know.'

'Well! I didn't! And that's that!'

Giselle didn't press the point. If Madame Tessier hadn't been so cantankerous, there would have been a better relationship between them all.

'I'll do it now,' Jean Claude offered, picking up the stool and setting it on its legs.

He felt the crunch of broken glass under his foot.

'That's the broken bulb. Have you another one?'

'In the packet, on the table.'

Whilst Jean Claude replaced the bulb, Giselle went into the kitchen, found a brush and dustpan and, once the room was fully lit, swept up the broken glass before anyone could cut themselves on it.

'What's going to happen to me, do you think?' Madame Tessier asked anxiously. 'Do you think I'll have to stay in hospital overnight?'

'It will be a bit longer than that, I'm afraid,' Jean Claude told her. 'This looks like a bad break. It will take weeks to mend!'

'But I can't be staying in hospital right now. My grandson is coming to stay with me for the holiday. It's only just over a week away. Do you think I'll be out by then?'

Giselle and Jean Claude looked at each other, both aware of the unlikelihood of her stay being that short.

'I don't think so,' Giselle told her reluctantly. 'You won't be able to walk on it for ages. Can't your grandson stay with anyone else?'

'There's no-one,' she said quite shortly, her expression hardening.

'What about his parents?' Giselle persisted. 'Even if you weren't in hospital, you really wouldn't be able to manage. You'll need careful nursing yourself!'

A few unbidden tears filled the old lady's eyes and she turned her head away. Giselle felt filled with compassion for her. She took hold of her hand.

'We'll think of something,' she said quickly. 'How old is he?'

'He's fifteen. He's a bit of a handful. That's why I said I'd have him.'

Her face was contorted with pain. She bit her lower lip grimly and Giselle could see she was fighting for self-control.

'Have you any other family? Anyone who would be able to help?'

Madame Tessier shook her head.

'Not since my Pierre died. These were his salt-beds you know.'

For a moment, her eyes held a faraway look as they shone with his memory, until the pain forced its way in again.

'We only had Marguerite, Alain's mother, and she . . . well, I may as well tell you. There isn't a father. She's a single parent.'

She said it almost defiantly, her eyes daring any comment.

'That's hard work, I bet,' Jean Claude said lightly. 'It's tough enough for two parents, especially these days, with so many temptations for young people.'

'Does she have to work?' Giselle asked sympathetically, carefully keeping her voice light.

'Yes, and she has to go on a training week at the time of the school holiday and is fearful of losing her chance of promotion if she cancels. Oh, dear! Whatever will I tell her?'

Giselle patted her hand.

'Don't worry about it. Look, I think I can hear the ambulance coming now. We'll come to the hospital with you, won't we, Jean Claude?'

'Yes, of course.'

'And we'll telephone your daughter once we know what is what, and I'm sure that, between us, we'll think of something that can be done with Alain for a week or so.'

The ambulance crew soon had Madame Tessier settled in the back of the ambulance and drove off to the nearest hospital. Jean Claude and Giselle followed in Jean Claude's car. After a detailed examination and X-ray, the doctor announced that the leg was broken in two places and needed immediate surgery. By this time, Madame Tessier was in shock and well beyond any comforting with well-meaning reassurances. She was very tearful and reluctant to sign her consent for what she saw as barrier to her being able to care for Alain.

Her daughter, Marguerite, arrived in time to sign the consent forms. She was a pleasant-looking woman of about thirty-five, obviously worried both about her mother and the problem her accident had created. She turned to Giselle and Jean Claude with gratitude after they had introduced themselves.

'Thank you for being so kind. I know

my mother isn't the easiest of people to get on with, and I don't know what would have happened to her if you hadn't been on hand. But, oh, dear! It would just happen now!'

Her face was creased with worry.

'Oh, but I can't be bothering you with it! You've been kind enough and I mustn't keep you. It's getting late.'

They shook hands, preparing to leave.

'I hope you manage to sort something out for Alain,' Giselle said as they turned to go. 'I'm sure you will.'

Marguerite made a wry expression.

'I'll try but it won't be easy. I don't suppose my mother told you, but he's been in trouble with the authorities. Anyone who was brave enough to take him on would have to sign a bond with the local police station and agree to various conditions for inspection visits and such.'

★   ★   ★

It was too late to go out anywhere. They found a late-night take-away and parked down at the port in Le Chateau D'Oleron, looking out across the narrow strip of water that separated the island from the mainland. At full tide, the sea was beautifully calm, totally at variance with the turmoil that the evening's events had created in Giselle's mind.

She felt the serenity of the peaceful scene seeping into her mind. Ever one to empathise with the underdog or those suffering misfortunes, she couldn't forget the hopelessness in Marguerite's voice as she had spoken the last sentence. What was Marguerite to do — look after her son and jeopardise her chance of promotion, or safeguard her career by making some makeshift arrangements for Alain?

'You know what?'

'Do you think . . . ' they both said together.

Then stopped, each waiting for the other to go on.

'You first,' Giselle insisted. 'You sounded more confident than I feel.'

Jean Claude took a deep breath.

'Well, I was just thinking that it shouldn't be too difficult to look after a fifteen-year-old boy for a week or so. After all, it's not all that long ago since I was one myself. What do you think?'

Giselle laughed.

'I was about to ask the same thing. It's a big responsibility though, especially with . . . well, you know, what his mother said about the police.'

Jean Claude half-turned away and gazed silently out of the car window. Giselle could see that his mouth was drawn into a tight line.

'Jean Claude?'

He turned to face her, nodding slowly.

'Yes, but not everyone in trouble with the police is bad beyond redemption. Maybe he deserves a chance.'

'Shall we offer then?'

Jean Claude nodded.

'Yes. There is one thing, though. I'd

rather not be the one to sign the bond. Will you sign it?'

Giselle expected him to say more, but he didn't, and she didn't feel she could press him to say more than he wanted to.

They made the offer the following day, when they met Marguerite at the hospital, where they had gone to make sure that Madame Tessier was settled.

'Are you sure?' she asked doubtfully. 'Though, I must admit it will take a lot of weight off my mind if you do.'

'Bring him over to see us and let's see how we get on,' Jean Claude suggested. 'We'll discuss what he is to do whilst he is with us. I think it will be best if we try to keep him occupied, don't you? I've been thinking of beginning to develop the section of the salt-beds that we bought with the land. I'm in the midst of discussions with Denis Perrotin about developing the area. Do you think Alain will be interested in helping? It will be hard manual work.'

Marguerite gave a hard laugh.

'I'll make sure he is!' she declared firmly. 'I think a bout of hard work will be the best thing for him! He's not a bad lad, but I do have to leave him to his own resources quite a bit and, well, he got in with a bad crowd. I know that doesn't excuse what he did but I think it will give him the chance he needs to make a break from the gang he got in with.'

'We won't be able to pay him much, but a bit of pocket money might encourage him.'

'That's more than generous,' Marguerite agreed. 'I don't think I'll ever be able to repay you. It really is good of you.'

'We'll need some help anyway, so it's beneficial to us as well,' Giselle assured her.

She and Marguerite hugged each other and then Marguerite shook hands with Jean Claude.

'We need to just pop in to see your mother now, and then be getting back to the restaurant,' Giselle explained.

'We're opening for a few hours late afternoon and early evening. We'll see you later then.'

Their brief visit to Madame Tessier wasn't quite as fruitful. She was very tight-lipped, though she mumbled her thanks for their offer to look after Alain. Giselle decided that she was too embarrassed by her earlier conflict with them and needed time to come to terms with their willingness to be of assistance.

The visit to the hospital prompted her to make her twice-weekly call to the hospital back home where her father was. She was encouraged to hear that the doctors believed that his unconscious state was at a much lower level than it had been. His body was responding to the slight electrical impulses in his treatment and they hoped for further good news within a few days. Giselle almost cried with the relief of it.

'He's going to get well!' she said to Jean Claude. 'I know he is!'

Her heart was much lighter as she made her preparations for the evening menus. She didn't expect the restaurant to be full each evening right away, so she had compiled a restricted menu, one that she could easily manage. She consulted Denis Perrotin about which wines to stock and agreed to a month's trial to giving him the contract as her supplier of wines, beers and spirits, agreeing with Jean Claude that supporting other local industries was a good policy.

During the afternoon before opening, she spent a hilarious half-hour training Jean-Claude to be a waiter extraordinaire! He quickly learned how to carry more than one plate in each hand without dropping one.

'How about this?' he asked, balancing a plate on one hand over his head, making a sideways step between two tables.

His cheerful smile made her heart flip. He was coming to mean a lot to her and she wasn't sure how to handle it. She wasn't convinced that his account of his career up to date was totally true or that he would be content to stay around for a longer term than the coming season, if he intended to complete the season at all. What sort of challenge would there be, once his salt-bed project was up and running? For all he described himself as a jack-of-all-trades, she was sure his real skills lay in something more specific, though, just what, she had no idea.

Realising Jean Claude was still waiting for her response, she pushed her thoughts aside and smiled.

'The ladies will come flocking in just to see you in action!' she assured him. 'I will have to make sure the food doesn't disappoint them, then they will come back for more.'

The evening was a moderate success. They served fourteen covers and received favourable remarks. Giselle was glad that there was no pressure to move people on and the diners seemed content to linger over their coffee and liqueurs, enjoying the peaceful atmosphere. More than half had chosen to eat out of doors, which again made the atmosphere more relaxed.

When the last few diners had departed, full of promises to return, Giselle and Jean Claude sank into two chairs and grinned happily to each other.

'Well, done, Giselle, Master Chef!' Jean Claude raised his glass in lighthearted salute.

'Well done, yourself!' Giselle retorted. 'You've made a big hit with your second career!'

'Third!' Jean Claude amended. 'Don't forget,' he said nodding towards the salt-beds, 'I'm also a property developer!'

'And what was your first career?' Giselle risked asking lightly.

There was a flicker of seriousness in his eyes, but it disappeared instantly.

'Like I said, an ill-spent youth,' he quipped. 'I'm now discovering my hidden talents and mean to make the most of them.'

Giselle still harboured doubts but she smiled back at him.

'Lucky for me!'

The following day, Marguerite brought Alain to see them. He was a tall, slim youth, typically French in his features and skin colouring, Giselle decided. He seemed agreeable enough and was pleased at the amount of money Jean Claude offered to pay him.

'We'll expect you to join in with whatever we ask of you,' Giselle warned, 'which will mean anything from digging the marshes out there to giving me a hand in the kitchen, or even out here.'

She gestured around.

'You mean waiting on tables?' he asked.

'Yes. Do you have any objections to that?'

'No. I think I might like it. I'll meet some classy girls!'

'I'd better watch out, then,' Jean

Claude said. 'For the two weeks you are with us, you can keep your tips, though if we ever have more staff, we'll probably decide to share them equally. Is that agreed?'

He held out his hand. Alain grasped it.

'Agreed.'

Giselle smiled. They were up and running, and had their first employed staff. She couldn't help a momentary twinge of sadness that her father wasn't there to share the moment but she recovered instantly. It would be something to tell him on the next tape she made.

# 7

The remainder of the week passed quickly. The number of diners varied slightly each night but didn't decrease and Giselle felt that they were making a fair start.

During the day, while Giselle was busy compiling the evening's menus and doing as much preparation as she could, Jean Claude continued with the outside painting that still needed to be done now that Ian had left them and he made good progress in his discussions with Denis over his projected plans for developing the salt-beds into a bird sanctuary and living museum.

In the evening, Jean Claude resumed his rôle as head waiter, building up an instant rapport with the diners. Giselle often caught his eye through the open hatch and pulled faces at him when he was charming the ladies. He merely grinned back at her, but the look in his eyes seemed to tell her that it was her who made his heart beat fast.

She was enjoying their light-hearted romance. It was as if he knew that she wasn't ready to make a full commitment, and she sensed that there was something holding him back as well. She sometimes wondered if it was another woman, but then she had never mentioned Daniel, had she? That was mainly because, she knew clearly now, there was no Daniel in her life. Her instincts in England, when he had wanted to make their relationship official, had been reliable. They would never be more than friends.

With Jean Claude, however, she hoped for something more, at the right time. At the moment, she wanted to get the restaurant on its feet and prayed to have her father fit and well again.

Every so often, they visited Madame Tessier in hospital, gradually breaking through the barrier she had put up between them. Noticing her obvious embarrassment whenever any slight hint of Marguerite's single status came into the conversation, Giselle began to wonder if her antipathy towards them stemmed from her knowledge of what had blighted her daughter's young adult life. It helped to explain her total disapproval of Jean Claude and herself sharing the cottage.

The following Saturday was busy. They were kept on their toes all evening. Giselle realised that, if the trend continued, she would need extra help in the kitchen before long and another waiter wouldn't go amiss. Their takings improved daily and Giselle wished she were able to tell her father in person how well they were doing, instead of just on the tape.

His vision for the place was being justified, and Giselle also admitted to herself that his desire to have her working there with him had been sound. She never had time to wonder what she would have been doing in Paris and if she had, she would have felt no regrets. It would only have been a step up her career ladder, whereas this was now her life.

Every day, Giselle's first waking thought every morning was that it was another day to live to its full. The island was in her blood and she loved it. At Jean Claude's suggestion, they didn't open on the Wednesday.

'We've earned a break,' he told her. 'Wednesday's our quietest day. Let's be tourists for a change, before the island gets swamped with the real ones next week.'

'Where shall we go?'

'Denis has a couple of bikes. Let's ride to the lighthouse and then work our way back, stopping off at all the small bays and coves. I used to do that when I was younger. My teenage version of a pub crawl!'

'And twice as healthy!'

They enjoyed it. The sun was shining and a gentle breeze was blowing. It didn't take them long to cycle the fifteen miles or so straight up to the island's most northerly point. They climbed up the steps to the top of the lighthouse overlooking the shelving rocky outcrop at that point. They ran across the low-lying landscape hand in hand, stopping only to poke in the rock pools and scoop up handfuls of seaweed to throw at each other — all of which ended with them in each other's arms, laughing and kissing!

After a pick-me-up at a small café, they set off on the serious business of cycling along the narrow, coastal road that twisted its way through small hamlets, with numerous short lanes that led off to the many beaches. They swam or merely paddled, dried off and went on their way. They had taken lots of fruit with them, which they ate for lunch.

By the time they reached the busy fishing port of La Cotiniere, it was early evening.

'I know a delightful restaurant,' Jean Claude confided. 'We're not really dressed for it but I think the head waiter will let us in.'

He did. He was one of Jean Claude's cousins! Jean Claude made known their need of a fresh shower, which Dominic was pleased to provide.

'And may I recommend our Japanese-style chargrilled plaice?' he suggested as he showed them to their table.

'No!' both replied in unison.

They turned and laughed together.

'No fish!'

It was getting late when they arrived back. Jean Claude lingered on the doorstep as he kissed her good-night.

'Do you want to come in for coffee?' Giselle invited.

Jean Claude nibbled her ear, but murmured, 'No.'

Giselle was torn between relief and disappointment.

'Why not?' she murmured back.

'We haven't got out chaperon to bang on the wall!'

Giselle giggled.

'So we haven't! She'd never believe it!'

A few moments later, she flopped happily on to her bed. Her body was deliciously tired, and she knew she was falling in love.

Alain arrived early on the Saturday morning. His mother dropped him off. They had shown her round on her previous visit and so, after giving Alain a few motherly admonishments about what his behaviour had better be, she bade him farewell, anxious to be on her way to her two-week course in Bordeaux.

Alain grinned sheepishly.

'I won't let you down,' he promised. 'I know what a fool I was and I've stopped seeing the other lads.'

'Good for you!' Jean Claude praised him. 'Now, I hope you've brought some old clothes, because we're clearing out one of the old salt-beds today!'

Giselle hadn't time to help them. She had added new dishes to the menu and, although she had made as much as could be safely frozen during the week, she had more than enough to get on with as regard to fresh products.

She called Jean Claude and Alain in to lunch and set down hefty portions of mussel and potato soup, accompanied by chunks of fresh bread and a selection of cheeses and salad. Both of them ate heartily, doing full justice to her cooking.

'I'll feed you two any time!' she joked. 'It's obviously a good recipe! It's my Soup of the Day so give it your recommendations, won't you?'

Alain followed her into the kitchen.

'What are those?' he asked curiously, looking at some trays.

'Canapés. Ever heard of them?'

He shook his head.

'No. Maman cooks all right, but nothing fancy. They're a bit small, aren't they? I'd need a bucket full of them!'

Giselle laughed.

'These aren't really part of the meal. I offer them whilst our customers are still studying the menu. They are intended to arouse the appetite, not to send it to sleep!'

'I don't think my appetite ever needs arousing!' Alain commented wryly. 'Maman thinks I've got hollow legs that need filling three times daily!'

'You can have some as a snack before you start waiting on tonight.'

She paused and looked anxiously at him.

'Do you feel OK with waiting on? We really do need you.'

He looked a bit sheepish.

'I've never done anything like that, but I'm willing to give it a go! It can't be too difficult, can it? Anyone can carry a few plates around.'

'Don't you believe it!' Jean Claude laughed. 'We've got more than half our tables already booked and we always seem to get a number of spontaneous diners! We'll be run ragged by the time we finish! I'll give you a bit of training before we start.'

Alain looked sceptical.

'OK,' he said and shrugged.

By the end of the evening, he was

more appreciative of a waiter's skills.

'How did I do?' he asked Jean Claude.

'Not so bad!' Jean Claude responded, with a sidelong grin at Giselle. 'He only spilled some soup twice and lost a basket of bread on to someone's lap! Oh, and took a set of meals to the wrong table! You were lucky! The people concerned were quite genial about it. Some would expect their meal free after such a blunder, with the cost out of your wages, young man!'

Alain was sleeping in the hut with Jean Claude, using the sleeping-bag and camp-bed bought earlier for Ian, so, after tidying up, Giselle left them to sort themselves out and made her own way back to the cottage, content with the way things were going.

It was a couple of evenings later that they first had any cause to regret their offer to take care of Alain. Giselle was busy cooking but became aware of some loud voices out on the veranda. Alain had taken some drinks out to some customers who had only stopped by for drinks. She realised that Alain was arguing with them and was about to go out when she realised that Jean Claude was approaching.

Some of the youths at the table were as tall as Jean Claude but fell back as he drew near. She could see him speaking sharply and gesturing them away with his arms. They eventually retreated, mouthing unpleasant threats. Jean Claude sent Alain inside, while he apologised to other customers.

'What was all that about?' Giselle asked.

Alain's face was bright red.

'They were some . . . er . . . mates I used to go around with. They were asking for chips and I was telling them we don't do chips. They got a bit out of hand and started calling me a stuffed penguin!'

He tried to smile but it was a false imitation.

'I didn't mind that so much. Names don't bother me, but I didn't want them to cause any trouble to you. I'm sorry.'

He looked very uncomfortable.

'Don't worry about it,' Giselle assured him. 'Jean Claude saw them off. I don't suppose they'll bother us again.'

She was wrong, however. The following afternoon she was alerted to more trouble by the sound of roaring motorbike engines. She stepped out of the kitchen to see six motorbikes being driven round and round the newly-made surface of the carpark they shared with Denis Perrotin. Alain was trapped in the middle of them, his face tense with anger and apprehension. Giselle ran across the bridge, intending to challenge the youths and send them on their way.

'Get out of here!' she yelled at them, knowing that her words would be unheard but also knowing that the expression on her face and the gestures of her arms would convey her meaning.

One motorbike drove straight at her

and she leaped aside, not knowing whether or not the rider would have stopped or swerved. Where was Jean Claude? Alain was looking anxious and was no more successful than herself in getting rid of the bikers. He made some attempts to dart out of the circle but the motorcyclists were driving too fast to allow him to make his escape.

Two of the bikers were making abrupt turns at the opposite ends of the carpark, churning up the hard-packed gravel, sending clouds of dust into the air.

It was this that first alerted Jean Claude to the episode. He was working at the far end of the salt-beds and had sent Alain back to get a fresh bottle of drinking water for them. He dropped his spade and ran along the narrow banks of the beds. The bikers continued their torment until he was only a few metres away, when, at a signal from one of the bikers, they all swung into line and roared off, tooting their horns.

Giselle was furious, and not a little

shaken. She stood, hands on hips, staring after them, feeling extremely weak at the knees. Alain was making his way towards her, his face red and looking very distressed. Jean Claude reached her first. He wrapped his arms around her, holding her shaking shoulders.

'Hey, come on. They've gone!' he cajoled, speaking lightly and looked over his shoulder at Alain.

'What was that all about? Were they your so-called friends again, Alain?'

Alain grimaced.

'I'm sorry,' he mumbled. 'They were taunting me because I've been avoiding them since my court case.'

'Do you think they'll come back?'

Alain shrugged.

'I don't know. Maybe, maybe not. They were reminding me about our gang motto, 'One for all and all for one!' You know, like the musketeers. We also had, 'Once a member, always a member'. There's no ending your membership!'

Jean Claude stared after them, though they were gone from sight, only the still settling clouds of dust reminding them of the disturbance.

'I won't ask you to tell me their names,' he told Alain. 'Not yet! But, if they give us any more trouble, I will change my mind! All I can advise you to do is to keep out of their way and do nothing to encourage them.'

Alain was subdued for the rest of the day. When he accompanied Jean Claude to the restaurant after changing into his dark trousers and white shirt, he stood uncertainly in the doorway. Giselle looked at him sharply.

'What's the matter?'

He scuffed the toe of his shoe against the wooden floor.

'I've been thinking,' he muttered. 'It's not fair to bring trouble to you. Maybe I'd better leave. If I leave the island, they won't know where to find me.'

'If that's the result of your thinking, I'd advise you not to do it too often!' Jean Claude responded. 'You can't leave the island! That really would put us in trouble, with the police and your mother!'

'And grandmother!' Giselle added.

That brought a flicker of a smile to Alain's face as he appreciated her sentiment. He shook his head, however.

'I don't know what they might do. No, I'd better go.'

Jean Claude grabbed hold of him by the shoulders and almost shook him.

'Alain! Have some sense, will you? You can't break your bond, and you can't land us in it! And think about your mother! She'd come rushing back here and we might as well have not bothered to help you in the first place!'

'I bet you're sorry you did!' Alain shouted back.

'No, we're not! But we will be if you throw it back in our face!'

'He's right, Alain,' Giselle intervened. 'It was nothing personal to you when we offered to help. It was for your mother and grandmother, but, now we know you, we want to help you. You're

126

doing all right here, isn't he, Jean Claude? Don't waste it! And don't let those yobbos spoil it for you either!'

Alain looked unconvinced.

'Don't say I didn't warn you,' he said, shrugging his shoulders. 'Well, I'd better get on with it, then. What d'you want me to do?'

'You can start by setting those tables.'

★　★　★

A busy time was approaching. Mother's Day had ensured that more than half their tables were booked out for Sunday lunch. With a restricted menu, Giselle knew she could cope.

As a speciality, Giselle had made special rose-shaped chocolate fondants as a gift for each lady and had ordered a few dozen red roses to adorn all the tables. Also, Saturday night had been busy and they were all tired.

'Straight to bed! It's a busy day tomorrow!' Giselle commanded as soon as they had cleared everything away.

She knew she would fall asleep as soon as her head hit the pillow.

She didn't know what had wakened her. She sat up in bed and listened hard. There was just the faint purr of a motorbike, growing fainter with each second. A motorbike!

Without a moment's pause, she leaped out of bed and rushed to the window. She dragged back the curtain and stared across the water. It was still dark, but there was a faint glow. It wasn't constant. It flickered.

Fire! The restaurant was on fire, and Jean Claude and Alain were sleeping next door!

# 8

Giselle leaped into action. She dragged on a pair of jeans and pulled a sweater over her head as she was making for the door. She ran as fast as she could across the carpark and over the bridge. She could hear a voice screaming, 'Fire! Fire!' and realised it was herself.

As she reached the first building, she began to bang on it as she ran, banging on the walls, banging on the window, banging and rattling the door.

'Wake up, Jean Claude! Wake up, Alain! The restaurant's on fire!'

It seemed ages, but it must have only been seconds, before the door was wrenched open and a bleary-eyed Jean Claude gaped at her.

'Quick, Jean Claude! Waken Alain! Get him out! The restaurant's on fire!'

As he took in her screamed words, his face underwent a visible change.

Fully alert now, he rushed back inside and half-dragged the struggling boy into the open. He pushed him towards Giselle.

'Get him fully awake. Here's my phone. Ring for the emergency services.'

He turned and ran towards the restaurant.

'Jean Claude! Don't! Come back!' Giselle screamed as she shook Alain. 'Are you awake, Alain? It's all right! You're not being attacked! It's me! Giselle!'

'What's happening?'

'The restaurant's on fire! Stay there! Don't move! No, better still, go to the roadway and wait for the fire engine. Direct them in!'

As soon as she saw him start off towards the road, she ran after Jean Claude. He was kicking away some burning rubbish that had been piled up against the door to the restaurant.

'Get back!' he ordered.

Giselle ignored him. She joined him

in stamping on the flames. When all signs of glowing embers had died away, they sank into each other's arms.

'Who's done this?' Jean Claude asked in bewilderment. 'It could have burned down the whole complex! And killed me and Alain into the bargain!'

Giselle told him about the motorbike she had heard.

'Of course, there's no proof it was anything to do with this, but it doesn't take too many brains to tie the two things together, does it?'

The sound of the approaching fire engine interrupted their musings. Giselle clapped a hand to her mouth.

'The fire brigade's here. I'd forgotten about them! They're going to think their journey has been a waste of time. Maybe I should have run here first. I'd have realised that we didn't need them!'

'No. We still need them to sift through all of this. We're covered by insurance but it's best to do everything officially. Besides, it's reassuring to know you thought of rescuing me and

Alain before the restaurant!' he added teasingly.

The fire brigade bore out his assessment of their rôle. They had high-powered flashlights to help them in their search and they damped down the hot embers. The fire chief took note of all their comments and promised to return on Monday to go through everything again in daylight.

'So, don't move any of the debris, will you? We need to have everything as fresh as possible.'

Giselle stared at him in dismay.

'But it's Mothering Sunday tomorrow . . . today,' she amended. 'We're more than half-booked. I've got everything prepared. We can't cancel!'

She turned to Jean Claude.

'What can we do?'

'Maybe we can use the other door,' he suggested. 'It's only this area we have to leave untouched, isn't it?' he asked the fire chief.

'Let's have a look.'

He studied the lay-out of the kitchen

and restaurant and decided that it would be safe to use the other entrance.

'But keep people away from this area,' he advised. 'The floorboards just here are quite charred. They could give way. You don't want to give your diners a ducking! I'd advise you to close off all the veranda, then there's no danger of anyone trying their luck.'

About a third of their tables were on the veranda. Giselle looked around with a frown.

'We can put some of the tables along the walk-way,' Jean Claude suggested, correctly reading her expression of dismay. 'And, if we don't accept any passing trade, we'll manage.'

And, manage they did.

It was a hectic morning. All three of them awoke sleepily but buckled to with the furniture removing. Fortunately, it promised to be a sunny day. Giselle left most of the moving of furniture to the two men. The kitchen was her domain.

They were all relieved when the last

customers had departed in late afternoon. All had been sympathetic towards them and no-one complained about the make-shift arrangements.

On Monday, after the fire chief had made his visit and departed, a local reporter and photographer arrived to cover the story.

'You'll make front page,' the reporter assured them. 'Look upon it as some free publicity.'

Both Jean Claude and Alain declined to have their photographs taken looking disconsolately at the charred door and floorboards.

'We're not as pretty as you,' Jean Claude joked.

The news spread locally and did indeed bring in a number of sightseers, all of which made for brisk trade. Ian was able to return for a day and their insurers gave them permission to make quick repairs. By the end of the week, it was business as usual. Alain left them at the weekend. His mother had returned from her course and expressed her gratitude towards them.

'Would you like to continue to work for us at the weekends, Alain?' Jean Claude asked the boy. 'That is, if it's all right with your mother and it won't affect your school-work.'

Marguerite was delighted.

'You've done him a lot of good,' she assured them in confidence, while Alain was collecting his belongings. 'I can tell already! He's lost his sullen look, and my mother is beginning to sing your praises, I can tell you! She's beginning to think her enforced stay in hospital has been a good thing. At least she's not making the lives of the nurses miserable by constantly demanding to come home!'

She was dismayed by the account of the fire. They had agreed to tell her. It had been in the local paper and someone was bound to mention it to her.

'And you are sure you still want Alain to work here? It might lead to more trouble.'

Giselle and Jean Claude were agreed on the matter.

'Once you start giving in to trouble-makers, they've won,' Giselle said lightly. 'Alain has worked hard and we really need him. We'll be taking on someone else soon, too. We'll be putting an ad in the local paper. Let us know if you hear of anyone, won't you?'

It seemed quiet without Alain on Monday morning but as all the weekend visitors had departed by the previous evening, Giselle knew that they could manage on their own for another couple of weeks. The beginning of July would mark the start of the real tourist season, and then everything would seem crazy!

Giselle received a letter from Daniel the following day. She read it with a sinking heart. He was coming out to visit her for two weeks. She really didn't want to have to face up to his constant pressures to become engaged. She had tried to let him know that her feelings for him were purely friendship but he

136

seemed to be oblivious to all she wrote. She sometimes wondered if he hadn't received her letters, for all the notice he took of them. Jean Claude took the news calmly.

'A special friend, is he?'

'No! Not as you mean!'

'How do I mean?'

'Like as in boyfriend? We were part of a foursome, but we all went our separate ways when our course finished.'

'Maybe he wishes to start up again.'

Giselle sighed. She knew that to be only too true.

'Where will he stay?' Jean Claude asked.

That was a problem! From what Daniel wrote in his letters, it seemed as though he was expecting to share the cottage and she didn't want that! Her face cleared. Thank goodness for Madame Tessier and her high-morality stand!

'Will it be all right if he shares with you, Jean Claude?'

Jean Claude grinned at her.

'I can stand it if he can.'

It was late on the Saturday when Daniel arrived. The restaurant was crowded. Giselle was busy cooking and it was the sound of his voice saying her name that made her look up through the open hatchway.

'Salut!' she greeted him, forgetting for the moment that he didn't speak much French. 'Hello,' she amended it and couldn't help responding to his cheerful smile.

Daniel leaned through the hatch, his lips pursed invitingly, obviously expecting a kissed greeting. Giselle leaned forward to give him a light peck but Daniel put his hand at the back of her head and held her there until she managed to squirm away.

'Daniel! I'm busy!' she hissed uncomfortably.

'Not too busy to give your best boyfriend a kiss, I hope!'

He turned round to include the diners in his remark, most of whom responded by banging the handles of their cutlery on the table. Daniel bowed gallantly, looking very pleased with himself, Giselle thought sourly.

'Want any help?' he then asked.

Without waiting for a reply, he went through the swing doors and took his lightweight jacket off and wrapped an apron round his middle.

'What needs doing next?'

Giselle didn't want him to help, but she knew she was being churlish.

'The next double order is grilled, stuffed trout and mackerel with lime and coriander. Both are to be served with a side salad and garnished with finely-sliced carrots and spring onions. You'll find the fish ready to be grilled over there.'

She had to admit that Daniel worked well with her. He always had. That was what had drawn them together in the first place but it didn't make them soul mates for life, she muttered to herself.

Every time Jean Claude came into the kitchen, Daniel seemed to be about to nuzzle into her neck or had his hands about her waist. Giselle could feel herself getting more and more tense.

'Behave yourself, Daniel! I can't concentrate.'

'I'm just making up for lost time, Giselle. It's been awful without you all these weeks. I can't wait until you come home again and we can get on with our lives! When's it to be, by the way?'

'Can we talk about it later, Daniel?' Giselle replied, not wanting to discuss it in the busy kitchen. 'It's been a busy day and I'm tired.'

'You've taken on too much! I told you so before you left England. Manuel over there's got the easier half of the job and has a skivvy to download on to.'

Giselle flushed with annoyance.

'His name is Jean Claude, as you very well know and he does very hard manual work in the day time. He's creating a bird sanctuary and cleaning up the salt-beds,' she added proudly. 'You'll be able to help him with some of the work.'

'Oh, no! I came out to help you, not him.'

He stood behind her and clasped her around her waist again, pulling her to him.

'As you say, we'll discuss it later, over a night-cap,' he whispered softly in her ear.

Before Giselle had time to respond, Daniel moved over to the cooker hob to attend to the grilling of the fish. Giselle sighed deeply. This was not going to be easy.

The diners seemed to want to linger for ever, ordering extra liqueurs and coffee. It gave Giselle time to do all the cleaning in the kitchen but she wasn't sure if that was good or bad.

'Come on! We can go now,' Daniel cajoled her, as the last diners left. 'Leave the paid staff to clear the restaurant! We've some catching up to do!'

'Jean Claude isn't paid staff. He's my partner and you know we always stay to the end. It's team-work.'

'Partner, eh?' he said, glancing across at Jean Claude. 'I hope that doesn't mean what I think it might mean.'

Giselle flushed.

'No, it doesn't! But we both help each other. He wouldn't be waiting on otherwise. He doesn't get any extra for it.'

'No? Well, you can tell he's an amateur. You can give him time off while I'm here. I'll soon get that youngster licked into shape!'

'Daniel! Stop it! We work well together but that's all it is. We're good friends. Stop trying to make it into something more.'

'Good! That's all I wanted to know. I was just a bit jealous, that's all. Come on, Giselle. I've driven a long way and I really am tired. I really do need to be getting to bed. It's after midnight.'

'What?' Giselle stared at him, her mind confused.

He had misunderstood her! She had meant she and Daniel were good friends, not she and Jean Claude!

'No, I didn't mean . . . '

'Hey, you guys! You don't mind if Giselle and I call it a day, do you?' Daniel called over to Jean Claude. 'We're all finished in here.'

'No, Daniel! It's all right, Giselle,' Jean Claude said calmly. 'I understand. Daniel has had a long drive on a hot day. Of course he is tired.'

He turned to Alain.

'It's late for you, too, Alain. Why don't you go with Daniel and help him to carry his bags to the boys' quarters and show him which camp bed is his? Sorry about the primitive washing arrangements, Daniel! We take turns to use the shower during the day.'

Giselle nearly choked at the expression on Daniel's face.

'It's in our tenancy agreement,' she explained, 'there being only one bedroom. I'm sure I told you in one of my early letters.'

'Well, yes, but we're almost engaged,' he said, dumbfounded. 'Anyway, your landlady's in hospital, isn't she? She wouldn't know!'

'No, but we would!' Giselle objected. 'And Alain's her grandson.'

She hesitated, wondering how to put it. If only he hadn't misunderstood her at her earlier attempt!

'You're pushing it, Daniel. I keep telling you, but you won't listen.'

She didn't want this, not here, in front of Jean Claude and Alain. She stood silently, biting her lower lip. Jean Claude stepped in.

'Look, we're all pretty tired and we need some sleep.'

He turned to Daniel.

'Sunday lunchtime is a busy time. I suggest you continue this conversation at a later date.'

'What's it got to do with you?' Daniel asked belligerently.

'Leave it, Daniel,' Giselle pleaded. 'Look, I'm glad you've come to stay. I've missed you and all our old gang,' she added hastily, in case he read too much into her words. 'Come on. Let's get your things and Jean Claude will help you settle in. I'll see you tomorrow morning when you come over for your shower and for breakfast.'

She was relieved when he heeded her words. The last thing she wanted was to fall out with him. She lay for a while, once she had gone to bed, worrying about the situation, but sleep overcame her before she had had any insight over how to handle it.

The following morning, Daniel was a different person. He was the first to come over, demanding cheerfully to know where the shower was and giving her an exuberant kiss on her lips.

'Sorry about last night,' he apologised. 'I was tired and things weren't exactly as I expected. I thought you might have missed me as much as I've missed you.'

Giselle laughed.

'I've been too busy to mope around, and I do so love being here. Dad was right. It is the right place for me. I just wish he were here, as well.'

'Will he get better?'

'Oh, I hope so. He's coming out of the coma slowly and, every time I ring, the doctors are getting more and more hopeful that he'll make a complete recovery.'

'Good. I shall hang on to that thought, then. But I'm not giving up on you, you know. Romeo over there had better watch out!'

'It's not like that!' Giselle protested.

'Hmm, if you say so! I could see the way he looked at you. He's jealous of me.'

'No, he's not!'

'What do you know about him, anyway? He doesn't strike me as being a full-time labourer, which is all he's doing here! What does he normally do?'

Giselle frowned.

'I don't know. Whatever it is, he's obviously taken time out for the summer. He's nice and we get on well together.'

'You don't seem to know very much about him! He could be anyone! A con-merchant!'

'I know his family and they obviously trust him to look after their interests!'

'Ha! There you've said it! Their interests! What about ours?'

Giselle looked at him sharply.

'There is no ours! This is Dad's business, remember!'

Daniel smiled disarmingly.

'No need to be so defensive, love! I'm only looking out for you and, as I said before, I'm not just going to walk away and leave the field clear for him. In fact, I might try to see what I can find out about him.'

'There's no need. I trust him.'

'You're too naïve, Giselle. You'd trust anybody, but I'm a little bit harder to please.'

# 9

The mid-week business began to pick up smartly and Giselle was relieved when Ian was able to come back to help Jean Claude repair the fire damage.

Daniel revised his determination not to work with Jean Claude, though Giselle feared it was because he would be doing his best to prise out of him any information about his past. She felt embarrassed by his lack of sensitivity and, although she was intrigued about Jean Claude's previous history, she was perversely pleased at Daniel's lack of success.

'Told me to mind my own business!' Daniel reported to her.

'I'm not surprised. I don't suppose you were exactly subtle, were you?'

'Well, he's hiding something. You can be sure of that.'

'Leave it, Daniel. As he said, it's none

of our business.'

Daniel's presence in the kitchen in the evenings made Giselle realise how hard she had been working and how much easier it was to have two of them working in there. Jean Claude agreed that they could afford to take on a part-time cook for evenings only on Thursdays and Fridays and the weekends.

'Once we're into July, we can increase her hours to cover the rest of the week and we'll get another part-time waiter until Alain returns for the summer holidays.'

Accordingly, Sylvie started to work in the kitchen a few days before Daniel returned to England, which gave Giselle time to asses and train her. She proved to be a capable, if unimaginative, cook and Giselle was satisfied with her. Berni, a classmate of Alain's, was started as a part-time waitress on Thursdays and Fridays. Alain was a bit put out.

'I could have done that,' he complained.

'We want you full-time in the summer,' Jean Claude explained, 'and this gives us a chance to see how Berni copes, without putting us under pressure. When you're working for us full-time, you'll need time off, since we won't be closing on Wednesdays in July and August. Otherwise, we'd be accused of overworking you. Don't forget, you're still under eighteen.'

On Daniel's last Wednesday with them, Giselle took him on a tour of the island, sharing her special places with him. He was lightly amused with her enthusiasm for them.

'You get too emotionally involved with places,' he criticised. 'It doesn't do to tie yourself to one place.'

'Ile D'Oleron is in my blood,' she replied quietly. 'Youngsters leave but most of them come back. Look at Jean Claude.'

'I'd rather not, if you don't mind,' Daniel said flippantly. 'Besides, he's hiding from something. He'll leave when it suits him. The island is too small for him.'

Giselle wondered if he were right. At the back of her mind she always thought he didn't fit the rôle of a casual entrepreneur whose main aim in life was to set up a bird sanctuary, however commendable that aim might be. Having had his name brought to mind made her reflect wistfully about their cycle tour of the island and their simple pleasure at being on the beaches and cycling along the coastal paths. Daniel simply wanted to head from one small town to the next, giving them scant attention. She supposed that it would be different if he had lived here, as Jean Claude had done, and, to her, of course, it was the scene of so many happy holidays.

Daniel's departure on the Sunday morning left her feeling slightly at a loss. They had been friends for almost four years but their closeness had gone. She felt Daniel was trying to recapture it but it didn't work, not for her at any rate.

Business was getting busier every day

and Giselle knew that, from the beginning of July, the two-month holiday season would be upon them with a vengeance. The climate on this particular curve of the French coast was the same as that bordering the Mediterranean. Practically every spare piece of land would have campers on it and the beaches, and roads leading to the beaches, would be crowded, with many of the visitors eating out.

Both she and Jean Claude had every intention of capitalising on the influx of visitors. By the middle of the first week in July, Sylvie was asked to work full-time and Jean Claude's sister, Christine, came to help out on Fridays and Saturdays. Alain was back with them full-time.

Jean Claude was pressing on well with his work in the salt-beds and had already cleared a circular route wending through the nearer one. He marked out the route with large stones, though he planned to create a series of information boards positioned at strategic points on the route, giving details of the varieties of birds that could be viewed from each location.

Denis Perrotin had stocked his wine cellar and benefited from the increase in trade engendered by the restaurant, as did a local cheese maker situated in another part of the small village. It was all good co-operation amongst local traders.

Giselle spent every morning buying fresh fish and other produce. She still preferred to buy the fish herself, often choosing something unusual if it was in the morning's catch, though she also bought herself a mobile phone so that she could, if necessary, telephone her orders through the wholesalers at the port. She had built up a reliable business with them and knew she wouldn't be short-changed.

She was glad she was so organised when, one Tuesday morning in the third week of July, Jean Claude took the wind out of her sails by telling her that he had to go away for a week or so. She stared at him, aghast at his statement.

'What? Just like that?'

'I'm sorry. It's out of my hands. I have no choice.'

He looked uncomfortable and had less than his usual composure. Giselle waited for him to say more but it wasn't to be.

'Can't whatever it is wait?' she asked desperately.

It wasn't just his waiting-on duties that she would miss. They worked at everything together and she knew she would miss his listening ear and sound counselling on any problem. Alain, Sylvie and Berni worked well but they were just what they were paid to be — hired help.

'Christine will come as often as she can,' Jean Claude promised. 'And she'll try to get someone to come in to do the washing-up.'

'I need someone else in the kitchen, too!' Giselle protested. 'It gets pretty hectic in there at times.'

'I'd noticed!'

Jean Claude grinned, making an effort to lighten the air, flicking a lock of hair out of her eyes.

Fortunately, all of the work force were willing to take their time off in the daytime and only rarely asked for a complete day off. September would be with them soon enough, with its accompanying fall in customers and lessening of working hours.

'When will you be going?' Giselle asked, trying to hide her dismay.

'As soon as I can get a flight, no later than Thursday.'

'Can I ask where you'll be going?' Giselle asked hesitantly, since Jean Claude wasn't being very forthcoming.

'London.'

'Right! Well, I hope everything goes well for you, whatever it is!' Giselle said, over-brightly.

She turned away hurriedly so that he wouldn't notice that her composure was about to crack. For a moment, she thought he was going to put his arms around her and wasn't sure whether it would be better if he did so, or better if he didn't. As it happened, he didn't and she realised he had gone out to start on his usual morning occupations.

She felt bereft, only then realising how totally she had come to lean upon him. Better she found out now than at the end of the season, she reflected, wondering again what exactly would happen when that time came.

Jean Claude got a flight from Bordeaux on the Wednesday evening. He chose to drive himself to the airport and leave his car with a friend of his who lived nearby. It was with a sad heart that Giselle bade him farewell. She felt as though the bottom had fallen out of her world and couldn't help comparing the way she felt to the milder sadness at saying farewell to Daniel a couple of weeks earlier. Daniel's words echoed in her mind.

'He'll leave when it suits him. The island is too small for him.'

Was that why he was going?

'Shall I phone you at all?' she asked hopefully.

After a slight hesitation, Jean Claude briefly replied, 'Only in an evening.'

He felt a heel, but what else could he say? He knew his manner was upsetting Giselle but he couldn't make it any easier for her, not without taking her into his confidence and that was impossible. He'd left it too late for that. He should have done so at the outset, except he hadn't known how things would develop between them.

He reached out and gently stroked his finger across her cheek, ending by tilting up her chin towards him. He could see that tears were brimming in her eyes.

'I'll be back,' he said softly, 'just as soon as I can.'

Giselle missed him in the days to follow. They all did, but there wasn't time to dwell on his absence, as they were extremely busy.

Christine was able to help on Friday and Saturday and had sent along a neighbour of hers for Wednesday and Thursday. Giselle felt tempted to ask Christine what had drawn Jean Claude away but didn't want to ask questions behind his back. It must be something he had no control over, or he wouldn't have gone, she was sure of that.

Saturday morning, Alain told her he had heard noises during the night.

'What sort of noises?' she asked.

'Someone outside. You know, trying the door latches and so on. I got up and had a look outside but couldn't see anyone.'

'You shouldn't have gone out. What if someone really had been there? They could have jumped you!'

'I had to make sure that they hadn't set a fire going again.'

'Do you think it was the same people?'

Alain shrugged.

'I don't know. If they know Jean Claude isn't here, they might come back.'

Giselle pondered on it.

'Anyone could be aware that Jean Claude is away. I don't see what we can do about it, do you? We'll just have to be extra vigilant.'

It was late when they finished on Saturday night. Berni said she had to leave straightaway as she had been late all week.

'Is your dad coming for you?' Giselle asked, knowing that she was collected each evening by her father.

'No, it's my boyfriend.'

'Oh, I didn't know you had one. Has he been in here?'

'No! Why should he?'

Giselle was taken aback by her impertinence.

'No reason. I'm only asking. We'll see you tomorrow then?'

Berni shrugged her shoulders.

'I suppose so.'

Giselle would have to keep an eye on Berni. She'd been larking about more than once since Jean Claude had gone and Giselle had threatened to replace her.

Shortly after Berni had left them, Giselle heard a motorbike. She ran to the doorway and just caught sight of the rear light as it left the carpark. She stared after it. Was it Berni's boyfriend? She pulled herself away and stepped back inside. She was becoming paranoid about motorbikes!

Alain, Sylvie and Christine set to help with a will and it didn't take them long between them to get everything tidied up. Christine and Sylvie left together.

'Do you feel all right being over here on your own?' Giselle asked Alain doubtfully, as she prepared to leave. 'I'm sure your grandmother would have no objections to you sleeping in my living-room.'

'No, I'll be all right,' Alain assured her. 'Maybe that's what someone wants — us both to be over there.'

'Don't! You're making me nervous!' Giselle laughed uncertainly. 'I tell you what. There's an old whistle in the kitchen. I don't know what it's doing there but you could keep it handy and blow it if you hear any strange noises.'

Alain agreed and Giselle locked up carefully, wishing for the umpteenth time that Jean Claude were here, or even Daniel. For the first time since being there she was feeling very vulnerable.

It was a long time before Giselle fell asleep and, when she did so, she slept fitfully, dreaming of intruders and break-ins. She suddenly realised that the noises weren't in her dreams and that she was wide awake. She glanced at her luminous clock. It was half past two. The sounds were coming from next door, from Madame Tessier's cottage.

Giselle listened carefully. Someone was definitely in there. She swiftly got out her mobile phone and rang through to the emergency services, giving an accurate report of the suspicious circumstances. The impersonal voice on the other end assured her that someone would be with her as soon as possible, and, on no account, to go outside.

Giselle crept to the window and looked out. At first, she could see nothing. Seconds, minutes ticked by. They seemed like hours. She fancied that she could hear the siren of an approaching police vehicle. Why did they always herald their approach? Suddenly, she saw movement. He was getting away! She instinctively ran to the door and pulled it open, ready to give chase. Then a police car, headlights full on swung round the corner and lit up the scene. The figure turned to face the headlights and stood rooted to the spot.

The car stopped and officers piled out, two running straight to Madame Tessier's cottage, another diving in a shallow tackle to pull the now running figure to the ground. There was a lot of shouting and banging inside the cottage and eventually two dark-clothed figures were hustled outside.

Giselle watched as in a dream as their anorak hoods were pulled back. The two from inside the cottage were one of the motorbike riders she recognised from the earlier incident inside the restaurant — and Berni! Giselle's mouth dropped open.

'Berni!' she breathed, aghast.

Berni tossed back her head and stared at her defiantly.

'You shouldn't have threatened to get rid of me,' she said sullenly, refusing to lower her eyes or turn away, until the officer holding her turned her round and hustled her towards the police car.

Her accomplice merely grinned round at everyone.

'Losers!' he shouted. 'All for one and one for all! Once a member, always a member!'

Giselle turned away. A shiver ran down her spine as she recalled Alain telling her of the gang's motto. Yet she wasn't prepared for the next shock. As the other figure was pushed forward towards the police car, her jaw dropped completely open. The other figure was Alain!

# 10

Giselle couldn't believe her eyes as she whispered 'Alain?' As if he heard her, though she knew he hadn't, he turned to look at her.

'I wasn't in on it!' he shouted across to her. 'You've got to believe me!'

He was hustled into the second car that had drawn up. Giselle didn't know what to believe. She simply stared at his retreating figure. One of the officers approached, notebook in hand.

'Mademoiselle Anderson?'

'Yes.'

'Is there anything you can add to what you said over the phone?'

She shook her head numbly.

'No, I don't think so.'

'You seem to know two of them. Can you tell me what is your connection?'

Giselle swallowed hard.

'They both work for me,' she said in

no more than a whisper, 'but I can't believe it!'

The officer laughed harshly.

'You'd believe anything if you had my job! Rob their own grandmothers, they would!'

Did he know how appropriate that statement was? Giselle shook her head.

'I'm sure Alain wouldn't! I think he was out keeping watch. He had heard noises last night but didn't see anyone. I should have known he wouldn't let it drop.'

The officer raised his eyebrows.

'I admire your loyalty but I think you'll be in for a disappointment. I know the lad. He's been in trouble before.'

'I know! That's what he's doing here! He's been working for us since the spring holiday. He wouldn't do this. He wanted to leave the gang. They've been pressurising him to rejoin.'

'You heard their war cry! Once a member, always a member!'

'Yes, but don't you see, they've done

this deliberately to involve him! Please question them carefully to give Alain a chance. I'd stake my reputation on him!'

'Hmm!'

The officer seemed unconvinced.

'I'll do what I can,' he eventually promised. 'Someone will come to board up that door. Don't touch anything in there until we give you the all-clear.'

With that, he returned to the second vehicle and they drove away, leaving a very subdued Giselle behind. She waited up until the man came to board up the broken door. He checked that all was secure and then he, too, left. She then had a drink of milk, still hoping for some sleep.

Barely was she in bed when her phone went. Not many people had her number and she hoped it would be Jean Claude, but that was too much to expect. It was Marguerite, Alain's mother, almost too upset to speak and wanting to know what had happened. Giselle told her what she had told the police officer and managed to calm her down.

'You will speak up for him, won't you?' Marguerite begged.

'Yes, of course, I will. Come round in the morning and we'll arrange to go to the police station together.'

That had to do for the time being and eventually Giselle fell asleep.

Sunday was a hectic day. Marguerite was allowed to see Alain, but Giselle wasn't. She returned to the restaurant to make what preparations she could for the lunchtime visitors, deciding to limit the menu to three items per course. Sylvie worked hard and Christine turned up unexpectedly, having heard about the break-in.

'I'll see you through lunchtime,' she told Giselle. 'That should help you a little. I'll come back in the evening if I can manage it, but I can't promise.'

Giselle was grateful for that. In the afternoon Marguerite also arrived.

'I must do an inventory for what might have been taken or broken from

Maman's cottage,' she explained. 'I do hope it's not going to land Alain in more trouble! He assured me he was having nothing more to do with the gang!'

'They couldn't have taken anything away,' Giselle told her. 'They were caught in the act.'

'What about Alain? Was he caught in the act, too? That's what the police think, isn't it?'

Giselle could only repeat her defence of the lad, even more convinced of his innocence. Alain wouldn't have let them down like that! She wished she could telephone Jean Claude but didn't feel able to do so. Whatever had taken him away must have been important. She couldn't help feeling let down, though. So many niggling thoughts kept buzzing their way into her head. Was he involved with someone else? Was he married? No! Christine or Uncle Thierry would have said! No, it was business, or something else of that nature.

They managed to get the lunches out and cleared away. After setting up for the evening dinners, Christine and Sylvie dashed home for a break with their families and Giselle began to do her preparation, preferring to keep busy than to take a rest. When the phone rang in mid-afternoon, she was almost relieved to hear Daniel's voice. At least there would be no complications from him that she couldn't deal with, but she was wrong.

'Where's Jean Claude?' were Daniel's opening words after his brief greeting to her.

'He's . . . er . . . gone to London for a few days,' she replied hesitantly, suddenly on the defensive. 'Why?'

'Did he tell you what he's doing there?'

'No. Why should he? You could say it's none of my business.'

'You could but you might change your mind when you hear this! He's one of the plaintiffs in a case of professional misconduct over a surveying scam that went wrong!'

Giselle's mind spun round. She barely grasped hold of the details that he filled her in with. Her mind was in shock. Jean Claude in a conspiracy to defraud? Had the world gone mad? It was as preposterous as Alain's part in the break-in! And did Daniel have to sound so smug about his revelation? He must know how much it would hurt her.

She knew she must have made some appropriate comments but she didn't know what and she blindly switched off the phone. She found her legs were shaking. It couldn't be happening. She wasn't sure she could face cooking dinner for twenty-odd strangers. She didn't know where to begin.

Christine returned first. Giselle challenged her about what she knew about Jean Claude's court case. Christine looked at her in dismay.

'How did you find out? Jean Claude wanted to tell you himself, when it's all over.'

'He should have told me before.

What's it all about?'

'He's been set up,' Christine told her. 'I don't know all the details but someone was fiddling the reports and either forged Jean Claude's signature or somehow got him to sign some hidden facts. He's innocent. I know he is.'

'And what if he's found guilty? What then?'

Christine looked downcast.

'He'll face a prison sentence.'

Giselle froze. It seemed as though her heart stopped.

'Fine! That's just what I need!'

There was only one good note. Alain was released on his bond and was allowed to return to work as long as he stayed with Giselle or his mother and didn't leave the immediate vicinity. The releasing officer gave them every reason to believe that they regarded Alain's version of the events as the true one. The other two suspects were put under a court order not to go within three miles of the restaurant until the case was dealt with.

Christine found another neighbour who would come in to help in the restaurant when Christine herself was unable to and they, somehow, managed to survive the next few days. Giselle found herself going through all the conversations she and Jean Claude had had, suddenly making sense of his reluctance to make long-term plans and being reluctant to talk about his past or have his photograph in the local papers. She wished he could have trusted her but realised that he didn't really know her at the start, and later? Well, when was the right moment to tell someone you were facing a court case?

'So, he was the surveyor who surveyed this place?' she asked Christine.

'Yes, but you needn't worry. He made a sound report and we backed him all the way.'

Giselle nodded. She had no doubts about it, not really.

She rang the hospital that her father was in, almost dreading more bad news.

Didn't they say it came in threes? Alain, Jean Claude and . . .

To her dismay, she was told to hold the line because the specialist wished to speak to her. She sank into a chair, not trusting her legs to hold her up if anything had happened to her dad.

' . . . and so he is asking to see you, Miss Anderson,' the specialist's voice broke into her panic. 'He has made a remarkable recovery over the past few days and is straining at the leash to be discharged. Of course, we can't do that immediately but . . . '

'He's all right? Are you saying that Dad's all right?' Giselle heard her own voice shouting down the phone. 'Are you sure? You're not just saying it?'

The doctor laughed.

'Yes, I'm sure! And no, I'm not just saying it! In fact, if you hang on, I'll transfer your call to the ward and you can talk to your father yourself.'

Giselle didn't know whether to laugh or cry. She did both while she waited to hear her father's voice and again whilst she was talking to him.

'Oh, Dad, Dad!'

'There, there,' he soothed her.

They talked briefly, a nurse's voice warning her father not to overdo it.

'When can you come and get me?' Tom Anderson asked his daughter.

'Oh, Dad, as soon as I can!'

She couldn't burden him with the problems that might prevent her coming for a few weeks. The restaurant couldn't be left, neither could Alain, but her dad understood.

'Keep the restaurant going strong, Giselle. I can wait!'

'But, I can't!' she said lightly, suddenly light-headed with relief. 'Oh, Dad, you've no idea how welcome your voice is to me!'

'I think I can imagine!' he replied dryly.

Suddenly, the sun was shining on her.

Daniel phoned again, keeping her up-to-date with Jean Claude's trial and was annoyed when she told him not to bother with any more details.

'I'll wait until he tells me himself,' she snapped at him. 'And that's that!' she said adamantly to Sylvie as she snapped off her phone. 'One boyfriend told where to go! And the other? Well, I'm keeping my fingers crossed for British justice!'

★  ★  ★

It was Saturday night, ten days after Jean Claude had left, nine since the break-in. Marguerite had managed to clear up the cottage and her mother was due out of hospital on Monday. They were planning a small party to welcome her home. In the meantime, their August visitors were every bit as numerous as those in July and with appetites just as hearty!

Giselle was hot and sticky. The steamy kitchen was not the best place to be on such an evening. She pushed a stray strand of hair behind her ear as she gently turned over the wing of skate in the grill pan. She'd be glad when the night was over and she could have a rest.

'Giselle!'

The voice startled her. It was Jean Claude's! She turned round and stared disbelievingly through the open hatch. Standing in the middle of the restaurant, in the midst of the crowded tables, was Jean Claude. But, it was the person at his side who brought tears to her eyes.

'Dad!'

She couldn't believe it! She handed the fish slice to Sylvie and ran through to the dining area as one in a dream. She was going to wake up and find she was in her bed! But the arms that clasped her were real and the tears she shed were real.

'Dad! I can't believe it! You're here at last!'

'Thanks to my partner here.'

He released her from his arms and stood aside to make the way clear for Jean Claude to step forward. Jean

Claude stood looking at her. He wasn't totally sure of his reception but the gleam in Giselle's eyes gave him hope.

'You're free?' she said hesitantly.

'Yes. My colleague broke down under questioning and I was completely exonerated. Am I forgiven for not telling you about it beforehand?' he asked. 'I just didn't feel I could lumber you with a jailbird for a boyfriend. You had enough to be worrying about with your father and the restaurant.'

Giselle smiled slowly and then ran into his arms.

'You're forgiven,' she murmured against his ear, 'as long as it doesn't happen again! No secrets from now on, do you hear?'

'Then I'd better show you this,' he said, drawing a small box out of his shirt pocket. 'It's something I bought in London for my favourite girl, hoping she'd say 'yes'!'

'Yes, to what?' Giselle asked, stepping back with her hands on her hips.

'We've been partners for four months,

Giselle, but I rather think your father will want to take over the main part of the business once he is fully recovered. I have a different sort of partnership in mind. I intend to re-site my surveying company here and work from home. Will you marry me, Giselle?'

A quiet hush descended over the restaurant, as everyone held their breath as they awaited her reply. Giselle was unaware of them. She needed no time to think. She knew how much she had missed him over the last ten days and didn't intend to let him out of her sight for a long time.

'Yes, I'll marry you,' she said and smiled broadly.

The place erupted in a crescendo of noise as the diners banged their cutlery on the tabletops. Tom called for champagne.

'To the future!' he toasted, beaming around happily.

And everyone agreed.

'To the future!' was the toast all round!